# So'Lan

## Book Four in the Galaxy Sanctuary Alien Abduction Romance Series

## Alana Khan

Temptation of the Horizontal Publishing, LLC

# Contents

# TRIGGER WARNING

The Alanaverse isn't filled with many rainbows and unicorns, although it abounds with happy endings. Here are some specific warnings.

Trigger warning

Trigger warning

Addiction is dealt with

A history of sexual slavery is mentioned with no specific details

End of trigger warnings

End of Trigger warnings

Want to be the first to see cover reveals, first chapters, and be eligible to win prizes and cool swag? Join my newsletter to get a few free books at www.alanakhan.com

So'Lan: Book Four in the Galaxy Sanctuary Alien Abduction Romance Series by Alana Khan

St. Petersburg, FL 33709

www.alanakhan.com

Cover by Elle Arden

# CHAPTER ONE

**P**resent Day
**Planet Fairea**

**So'Lan**

"Are you ready to look in the mirror?" Pherutan, the medic, asks with a smile. "How long has it been?"

He's trying to be kind, but I'm irritable and don't care for small talk. He's wondering how long it's been since my former master yanked my fangs from my mouth to punish me.

"Time lost meaning in that underground dungeon. I think I was there three *annums*."

"I didn't realize you'd been there that long. The one *annum* I was there felt like an eternity. That you survived that hell for three *annums* is a testament to your spirit and tenacity.

"I'm sorry I've made you wait so long for this," he says. "I wanted to give your body time to heal from all the trauma so your implants would graft well."

Maybe it's that I'm long overdue for my pain medicine, but he's annoying the *drack* out of me. I humor him, though, and walk to the mirror in the refresher.

I was not a humble male. In my prime, people shouted my name in arenas from Aeon II to Xenon. It echoed in my ears like thunder. I was a proud male. Some would say egotistical. I was on my way to becoming a Pinnacle fighter, one of the best in the galaxy. Indomitable.

Then a series of mishaps—a lingering infection that traveled to my heart, and an ill-timed gladiatorial match—combined to result in a string of losses. Those losses angered my owner, Daneur Khour, the psychopathic boss of the MarZan cartel, and I became the focus of his displeasure.

To incentivize his other fighting stock, he threw me into a dungeon on his property, pulled my teeth, tortured me in other more insidious ways, and starved me until I was *hoaras* away from death.

There were others in that underground torture chamber who had the misfortune of displeasing our sadistic master and had to endure his abuses. My spirit had died along with my will to live but I couldn't take my own life as I wanted to. Any attempt to end our own suffering or failure to comply with any of his edicts resulted in punishment for everyone. I wouldn't allow myself to put them in harm's way, so I endured.

As gladiators, slave or free, no matter what planet we are from, we are brothers. Slaves are forced to fight and kill each other in the arenas, but outside of those venues, there is an unwritten code of honor that we would never intentionally inflict harm on each other. So we all suffered in silence and ate and drank the meager rations that barely kept us alive.

When I look in the mirror, I see it all. Where before the mirror reflected a handsome Ton'arr male, what the Earth females describe as lion-like, now I see only the shadow of who I was.

I've regained most of the weight I lost. The flesh and fur that hung off my emaciated form have now filled out. Good nutrition and Pherutan's specially formulated tonic have miraculously sped up my physical healing.

I've worked out in the *ludus* for the last few *lunars* and although I'm not in shape to fight a gladiator bout, the good news is that I don't need to. I'm free. But if you look into my eyes, or note the tight set of my mouth, it tells the story of the misery I've endured.

I snarl at the mirror, flashing fang for the first time in *annums*. Having my fangs back, even though they're only implants, should ease my heart. But it doesn't.

"Well?" Pherutan asks. "Do you look like your old self?"

My old self is dead.

"Yes. Thank you." I pause, knowing what I'm going to ask next is going to be a hard sell. "I've run out of pain medication."

His distressed sigh floats in from the other room.

"So'Lan, you've been out of the dungeon for *lunars*. You've almost returned to your optimum weight. Your body has recovered. You don't need pain meds anymore."

Anger flashes through me so swiftly I can't control the roar that bursts forth. It was so loud and long that after it's over some of his instruments are still vibrating against the metal table.

I return to the exam room from the refresher, too angry to apologize.

"Do you live inside my fur?" I thunder. "How dare you assume you know my level of pain?" I walk too close to him and let an aggressive feline rumble rise from the back of my throat. He's a smart male. He knows it's a warning.

"I'm not a doctor, just a medic. You should know this. We were in that dungeon together for an *annum*," he says as he takes a step backward. "My scans show you've made a full recovery. Perhaps you should go into town and see someone more qualified."

Anger flares through me again. It's white-hot and out of control. I'm barely aware of what I'm doing until I realize I've cornered him in his own medical room. I tower over him by half a head.

He's a gladiator as were all eight of us who were the last ones left in the underground dungeon. We were all so weak, abused, thirsty, and starved when we were rescued, we had to be helped up the steps. I was the only one so near death I needed to be carried.

Pherutan was never on his way to greatness. Perhaps it was lucky he was jailed in the dungeon. If they'd left him above ground to fight more matches, he'd probably be dead. He likes to read. He's studying to be a better medic. This male wasn't built to be a gladiator. Maybe his physique, but not his mind.

I loom over him, give him another threatening feline chuff, and dip my head level with his face, staring at him. Daring him to argue.

"I couldn't give you more meds if I wanted to, So'Lan. We're out."

I roar in his face so loudly he flinches.

"What about the med kit in the kitchen?" I ask. My mouth, no longer fangless, is inches from his.

"Someone cannibalized it weeks ago."

He smartly doesn't accuse me of doing it, although we both know I did.

"You didn't replenish it?"

"We were already running low," he says with a swallow.

I give a warning growl as my muscles tense. My reactions are spiraling, becoming increasingly out of control. If I don't get a handle on myself, I might hurt this male.

Shaking my head, I try to compose myself. I'm not like this. My behavior has become erratic. I'm not proud that I just backed a brother gladiator into a corner in his own territory.

The angry roar that again erupts from my throat surprises us both.

Dhoom and Abraxx burst through the door. That they're shocked is obvious by their open mouths and wide eyes. When I follow their gaze, I see my fist is gripping Pherutan's shirt at his collar, his feet dangling as I hold him off the floor.

"What's going on?" Dhoom asks, his hand on a laser pistol at his belt.

Ten *minimas* later, we're in Dhoom's office. I'm sitting in a chair against the wall across from his desk, flanked by Abraxx on one side and Thran on the other. Naomi is standing along the side wall next to Pherutan. My mind casts back in time as I review the events that brought me here.

Several *lunars* ago, a band of gladiators came to kill Khour, the head of the cartel. It seems many people in the galaxy wanted him dead as much as I did. They completed their mission, and by a stroke of luck, they stumbled onto the well-hidden underground dungeon where seven brother gladiators and I were imprisoned.

Five women were being held on the property, as well. All human. The gladiators who rescued us set us up here with forged papers, which gave us ownership of the entire compound. We named it Sanctuary.

We've reclaimed the place and cleaned it up after the intense battle we fought with Khour's lackeys. We're growing crops, raising egg-laying *prens,* and meat-producing *anlaks*. We want Sanctuary to be a beacon of safety for slaves running from their masters.

I scrub my face with my hand when I admit the truth to myself. When I say "we" reclaimed this enormous compound, what I mean is "they."

After my rescue, I was far too debilitated to function. Parasites had leached all health from my body. Between the forced starvation and ill-health, I'd lost a hundred *dextans* of weight. I was bedridden for weeks after our rescue. I wanted to die. I was completely demoralized. Pherutan strapped me to the bed and pumped in anti-parasite medication, nutrition, steroids, and painkillers through tubes in my arm and stomach.

Something changed after we celebrated Blessed Peace Day with many friends of Sanctuary. A tiny spark of life rekindled in the spirit I thought was dead. I started taking the tonic from Pherutan and began to exercise in the *ludus*. I won the battle against my physical body. The emotional battle is far from over.

When I'm not exercising alone in the *ludus*, I pace in my room in the males' dorm, or stalk around the compound watching them work. I get jittery if I don't get my pain pills on time. I don't want to admit it, but Pherutan was right. I couldn't tell you where my pain is if you demanded it of me. I just know I ache.

Naomi and Pherutan take seats against the wall. Their gazes flit from mine when I stare at them. Dhoom glowers at me from behind his desk. The two gladiators flanking me shift uncomfortably in their seats.

"Pherutan brought his concerns to Naomi and me a few weeks ago," he says, his voice stern but calm.

He and Naomi have leadership roles at Sanctuary. Dhoom deals with male-related issues. Naomi loosely oversees the females and much of the financial concerns. Normally, Naomi wouldn't be here, it would be considered Dhoom's domain. That she's been called in to help decide my fate doesn't bode well for me.

"Do you want to discuss things? I'm happy to talk," he offers.

My ears prick with excitement. Perhaps my little outburst in the medic's office will earn me a sharp talking to. After, I can secretly rummage for pain pills in the med kits in the spacegoing vessels.

"I'm happy to talk," he repeats, "but let me cut to the bottom line. You need to stop using the medicine. It's addictive. It's so addictive it's become the drug of choice all over the galaxy. I don't care what the medical name for it is. We all know what it's called on the street. Synth. I won't allow you to keep using it. Look what it's done to you, So'Lan."

He frowns as he steeples his fingers under his chin and leans forward.

"We were in that dungeon together for a long time. I know you for the male you truly are. You were the glue that kept us together down there.

The male whose pep talks kept us alive. I'm proud to call you my friend."

He spears me with his sincere, red-eyed gaze.

"It just goes to show what that *dracking* med is capable of. You aggressed on Pherutan. Almost attacked him. We can't have that."

"Don't worry," I grumble. "Our esteemed medic tells me there's none left in the compound."

As these words leave my lips, I realize I could easily hover east, to the enormous fair and snag some Synth from the black-market vendors there. I'm surprised that didn't occur to me earlier.

"A shipment is on its way here. We need to have it on hand for its medicinal purposes. It should have arrived by now. I don't want to have to lock it up, So'Lan. Pherutan advises and both Naomi and I agree— you need to detox." Dhoom looks pained to have to tell me, but by the firm set of his mouth and his steady stare, he will not change his mind.

"That's going to be a problem," Pherutan interrupts as he looks up from the data pad in his hands. "I've been researching procedures. If we'd had this talk yesterday, I would have been fine with following the detox protocols here on Sanctuary.

"What just happened in my medbay showed me you're too far along, So'Lan. You need twenty-four *hoara*, supervised medical detox."

I roar. It flew out of my mouth before I could stop it. The males to my right and left leap to their feet, their hands on their sidearms. They look at me in shock, but their steady hands on their stun guns tell me they won't hesitate to use them if they have to.

They came into this meeting armed. Are they right? Am I really this far gone?

"You can't detox on your own, So'Lan. We could handle you here if it was just the relatively mild symptoms of agitation, anxiety, muscle aches, sweating, shakes, and runny nose. But watching you today? The unleashed anger and possible seizures? You'd be safer in a facility that specializes in this. The best facility in the sector is on Kryton," the medic continues. "The planet is known for its medical facilities. I suggest we get you there right away."

I gauge the distance to the door, even as I wonder where I would go from there. I have my comm bracelet on. It's loaded with credits. We've all been paid a wage every *lunar*, although I've done little to no work. I could make my way to the fair, buy Synth.

My friends pity me. They're looking at each other like they share a secret. The secret that I've lost my mind.

"Excuse me," Melodie interrupts over comms. "The vessel *Serenity* is asking permission to land. The pilot says Captain Thantose of the pirate vessel directed them here to pick up the Dacian statue."

"Yes," Naomi says. "We're selling it on the black market. It belonged to Khour. We're only getting thirty cents on the dollar, but Thantose found a buyer and beggars can't be choosers. He contacted me and said he was in another sector. Sent a friend he said we could trust to pick it up and deliver it to the buyer. Tell the *Serenity* they can land."

"So'Lan," Pherutan returns to our conversation. "You need to go to treatment. I want you to go today."

"NO!" I roar, flashing my new fangs.

"Look at yourself, my brother. This isn't you. You have a family here. People who care. Let us help you."

"NO!" I roar again, lunging, then snapping at Dhoom.

I don't see Abraxx activate his laser stunner. It brings me to my knees. I try to roar, but it comes out as a strained grunt. I stay where I am, knowing that if I try to get up, the next laser burst will be on a higher setting.

## Phoenix

The amount I'm making on this run is barely enough to keep me in fuel and make a partial payment on my runabout. At least it's work. And this cargo isn't high profile, so I won't have half the galaxy trying to intercept me before I get to the buyer on Kryton.

"Cleared to land," the female voice informs me. My translator didn't have to perform. She's speaking English.

Captain Thantose must know every human female in the galaxy. He has three on his pirate ship, including his mate, Brin. He must have a soft spot for Earth girls—he saved my life several years back. And these little jobs he throws my way are keeping me in credits. I guess I shouldn't resent the meager income. It sure beats my previous occupation. Sex slave.

I set the *Serenity* down where Melodie instructs—right in the middle of the property. There's a human female standing in the doorway of a low-slung structure that appears to be an office building. She's waving at me. That must be her.

The compound seems built around an ancient well. There's a mansion, or maybe it's a castle, toward what appears to be a forest. Buildings of various sizes ring this central area. They all look like someone slightly high on marijuana designed them. They're built of rose and beige checkerboard stones. It's slightly whimsical while being fully functional.

"Hey, I'm Melodie." She raises on her toes and waves again. "Thantose sent word. He said you were from Earth."

I usually keep my head down while I'm picking up and dropping off merchandise. It's not safe for Earth women out in space. So I lie about my origins and insist I'm from Morgana since Morganian females look identical to Earth females. But since Thantose said Sanctuary was full of human women, I allow myself a moment to enjoy hearing my native tongue and seeing a face that looks a lot like mine.

"I've been told to escort you to Dhoom's office right away. Maybe afterward you can join us for dinner?" She glances back at my ship, then tilts her head and asks, "Where's your crew?"

"I travel alone. Doom?" I ask, my eyes wide. Maybe I should draw my blaster.

"Oh." She chuckles. "I don't know what it means in his language. It doesn't describe his personality. Don't worry. You're safe here. If it will make you feel better, I'll stay with you."

After we enter the building, she leads me down the hallway. When she opens the door, my head tips back in surprise.

"It's not what it looks like," a fortyish human female tells me as she rises from her chair. "I'm Naomi. We've had an… event. Don't worry."

Don't worry? There's a lion-man kneeling on the floor with two weapons pointed at him. By the deadly look on his face, he's planning to tear us all to shreds with those dangerous-looking fangs of his. To describe the scene as tense is an understatement.

He's half humanoid, half lion. His nose is wide and flatter than a human's. It's surrounded by whiskers. His piercing blue lion-like eyes don't have slits, but now I remember lions don't have that kind of feline eyes. Their pupils are round.

His mane is striking in contrast to the golden fur covering his muscular body. It's thick and long and a deep chestnut color. The same thicker, darker fur is on the tuft of his tail and forms a V from the center of his broad shoulders to the middle of his chest.

"How would you like to earn yourself some additional credits?" Naomi asks. I like her already. She knows exactly what this looks like and doesn't even try to hide it. She cuts directly to the bottom line, and the bottom line is money.

"Yes," I answer her directly. Naomi and I will negotiate this straight.

"You're taking the statue, the Dacian bust, to planet Kryton?" she asks, although she knows the answer. She's the one who brokered the deal.

"Yes." I don't ask questions. She's smart enough to know what information I'll need in order to make a decision, and she's not going to tell me anything extra, even if I ask.

"This gladiator needs to get to the Shining Star Facility there. Everything's been arranged. You're going to Kryton anyway. How much to take him as a passenger?"

If looks could kill, I'd be dead. He's staring at me. His deadly blue eyes seem to be assessing how fast he could leap up and tear out my carotid with his gleaming white fangs.

I take two steps back. "He doesn't look like he wants to come with me, and I value my life." Speaking of carotids, mine is leaping in fear at my throat.

"We'll give him a sedative," Naomi explains calmly, as if we're having a normal conversation. As if there's no huge, angry lion-man looking like he's planning to have us both for dinner.

He roars and seems about to rise to his feet, but all four males in the room point their weapons at him and he sinks back onto his heels.

"What's the deal? Aren't there any *facilities* on planet Fairea?" My shit detector is screaming at me, klaxons are ringing in the back of my head, and red flags are being thrown in the privacy of my mind. This guy is bad news. Facility? Is that another word for jail?

"It will be a simple surgical strike. Get him into your vessel. Fly him to Kryton. Upon proof that you've delivered him to the facility, twenty thousand credits will be deposited into your account. Piece of cake." She gives me an attempt at a smile. It's a fail.

Whew. For a moment there, I thought I was going to have to make a hard decision. I wondered which would win out, greed or common sense. An offer of only twenty thousand credits? The decision is easy.

"Sorry. No can do. Do you have the bust? I gotta bounce." I put my arm out, palm up, as a visual aid. My meaning is clear: gimme the goods, I gotta get on my way.

"It's a simple drop-off," Naomi says matter-of-factly. "He's not wanted for any crimes. He'll just be a passenger."

Okay. Now I'm pissed. I stalk to her and get up in her grill although she's a tall woman and I'm not.

"I'm not stupid. This is not going to be a simple in and out. I have eyes in my head. And with those eyes as well as my other spidey senses I've observed the following. One, there are four males in here, all built like fucking gladiators, and they're all on high alert with their weapons drawn.

"'Piece of cake' is not an adjective to define a three-hundred pound lion-man gladiator with…" I turn my head to examine him, "with gleaming four-inch fangs."

"Three… never mind. All I need is the first two. Oh, and 20,000 credits? That's insulting. Do you still want me to deliver the bust?" I put my hand out again in a gimme motion, waiting for the goods I'm supposed to fly to Kryton.

The guy behind the desk looks like he wants to try his hand at the negotiation. I've been in space for almost ten years. I'd say he ranks as one of the scariest fuckers I've ever met. He not only has a brilliant red topknot, but his red eyes are piercing right through me.

"He's a fellow gladiator, a beloved comrade," he says without a hint of sarcasm.

I don't laugh, although there's a snarky part of me inside rolling her eyes. *This* is how you treat a beloved comrade? Loaded weapons aimed at his heart? And why would this asshole be called beloved when he's roaring, flashing his fangs, and clearly looking for a way to tear everyone in the room limb from limb?

"I'm Dhoom," the red-eyed male says.

Of course he is.

"He's an honored male. We've treated him with respect. He's had trouble recently. Both of our spacecraft are out on missions, or we'd take him ourselves. We need your help. Just name your price. It's urgent he gets treatment immediately."

His gaze darts to Naomi and there are ten volumes of unspoken discussion as they argue with their eyes. The theme music from Saturday night fights is playing in my head. Dhoom's blazing red eyes just told Naomi to go fuck herself. He's going to get his friend the help he needs, no matter the cost. By Naomi's pursed mouth and her eventual glance at the floor, I think he won.

Which means it's Phoenix's lucky day. I think he just gave me carte blanche. Today's looking better all the time. She offered 20,000? Hmm. "120,000," I say even as I decide I'll go as low as 100,000.

"Done," Dhoom says. "We'll give him a sedative—" The beloved comrade roars so loudly it hurts my ears. I slip my sidearm out of its holster and now there are five weapons pointed at the animal-man still kneeling on the floor.

"So'Lan," Dhoom's deep voice booms over the ear-splitting, vicious roars. "This is for the best," he says as my heart flutters against my ribcage.

As if they'd practiced it, three males approach him, weapons drawn, while the fourth throws a net over him. They work in tandem, taking him all the way to the floor. When he's lying on his belly, the medic who threw the net gives him a syringe full of sedative. The beast-man chuffs once, twice, three times, then every muscle in his body slackens, his eyes flutter closed, and he loses consciousness.

"Deliver him to the treatment center first," Dhoom says, "before you deliver the bust. We care about this male. We're a family here at Sanctuary."

The medic gives me ten pre-filled syringes. "These are sedatives. They're good for eight *hoaras* each. There are twice as many as you should need."

"You're sure he'll remain unconscious for the entire trip?" I ask as I pace a full circle around him. He's powerful. A gladiator. If he got loose on the journey, I wouldn't even qualify as a snack. I'd be dead in an instant.

"We'll carry him and secure him to one of the beds." Dhoom pauses, then says, "I assume you have more than one bed."

My vessel is small, barely the size of a minivan, although it has a large cargo area underneath for the illegal goods I haul around the galaxy. It only has one bed.

I shrug. For 120,000 credits, I'll sleep sitting up in my seat. "How secure?"

"Wrist and ankle cuffs. Don't worry. He'll be knocked out the entire time."

Everything about this is hinky, even the 120,000 credits. Strike that. *Especially* the 120,000 credits.

"Look." I walk to the lion-guy and nudge him with my toe, then stare at Dhoom. "Someone needs to spill it. I need to know what I'm signing on for or the deal's off."

Melodie, the female who walked me here from my vessel, has been standing in the doorway the entire time.

"The guy on the floor is So'Lan. His species is from Ton'arr," she says as she edges into the room. "Dhoom's right, he's well respected. He's been very ill. He almost died a few months ago. Since then, he's developed a little Synth problem."

All the gladiators suck in a breath, as if they're shocked at her blunt words. No one is more shocked than me. Synth. Shit.

"The guys try to pretty it up, but all of us Earth girls know what's been happening. They call it a painkiller and use pharmaceutical grade medication, just like they did with opioids on Earth, but it's addictive as hell, and So'Lan is hooked. I'm not privy to exactly what happened today." Her eyes flick to the golden male on the floor, still bound by the net, although he's unconscious. "But I think he just had an intervention —an unsuccessful one."

She looks pointedly at Dhoom and Naomi. When Dhoom nods, Melodie says, "I've been watching, and listening, from afar. If he wakes up on your vessel, he's going to be in a bad mood."

In my mind, I see a cartoon version of a pile of money with wings flying out the door. This lion-man is going to wake up in an hour or two on my vessel in a bad mood?

The words "bad mood" are for overtired children. This guy? With his four-inch fangs? I think pissed as hell or loaded for bear are better descriptors. No. How about lethal?

"Forget it. Wait until your own starships get back and take your venerated, honored, pissed-off hero to detox later," I say ruefully. Damn, that fat pile of credits was almost in my hands.

"He's going to go into withdrawal in," the male who is obviously the medic inspects his wrist-comm, "twenty *hoaras*. He needs to leave now. We'll secure him well. You'll have the sedatives.

"You'll keep him comatose until you arrive on Kryton. I'll connect him to an intravenous concoction that will provide nutrition and fluid that is 100% absorbed, so voiding won't be necessary. He'll never even know he was aboard your vessel. He'll be safely in his bed at the Shining Star Recovery Center before he knows he left planet Fairea."

The corners of my mouth curve downward as I try to talk myself out of this. It's a terrible idea.

"150,000 credits," Dhoom offers.

Here's a male who speaks my language. Until he upped his offer, I was ready to bounce.

"How do I say no to that?" I say as I offer my hand to Dhoom, waiting for him to shake. "I'd be honored to take your venerated friend to Kryton."

# Chapter Two

**P** hoenix

This little job has certainly exceeded expectations. I'll hit Kryton's atmo in less than six hours, and this whole excursion will be in my rearview mirror.

Rather than wait the full eight hours between administrations, I've given them at six-hour intervals. He's been so out of it the entire time, his eyelids haven't even flickered.

I haven't given him a lot of thought on the trip. I've been thinking about upgrades I can make to the *Serenity*. Maybe I'll just pay her off. I don't want to be in hock to Thantose anymore. With the 150,000 credit payday, this little beauty will be all mine.

So'Lan moans. I've waited a bit too long to give him this last dose. I shake my head when I look at him. Just what the galaxy needs. Another angry, pissed off guy who thinks the world owes him sympathy because his life sucks.

"Sorry, So'Mad, you're going to wake up in a treatment facility." I imagine it will be cushy. The way those males acted, this jerk is like royalty to them. I doubt he'll get the presidential treatment on Kryton, though. Detox is hell no matter how cushy the bed is.

I can't wait to touch down at the Shining Star Recovery Center, unload my feline cargo, and collect my credits.

"It's been a pleasure to have you onboard, So'Sad," I say in my best approximation of a stewardess. "Glad you chose to fly the friendly skies of the *Serenity*."

We've been squished in my tiny runabout for almost two days, I've given him eight shots, and attached two new bags of magic liquid to the IV running into his arm, but I've never really paid much attention to addicted Mr. Venerated Gladiator here.

The last bag of fluid just emptied, so I remove the IV needle and dab the spot on his arm to stop the bleeding, just as the medic instructed.

Melodie said he was from planet Ton'arr. They must be isolationists. I've never seen this species in my interstellar travels. He's an interesting combination of humanoid and lion. The mixture is striking. Handsome.

Well, handsome and scary. Those teeth would definitely strike fear into anyone with a brain if they were attached to the mouth of someone angry. Glad I'm never again going to see So'Scary when he's awake.

His fur is golden. The rich chestnut mane is striking as it sweeps to the back and down his throat to a V on his chest. He has little black dots where his whiskers emerge from near his flattened nose. His fur-covered rounded ears are high above his temples. Regal.

I should let sleeping dogs lie, or in this case, sleeping felines, but out of curiosity, I touch one of his humanoid fingers. When I press behind the nail bed, I see a sharp feline claw emerge. Mother nature was generous to the Ton'arr. She gave them some good self-defense mechanisms, as well as making them attractive.

Shit! I see something out of the corner of my eye. When I turn to look out the nav screen, I see meteors barreling right at me. Dozens of them. Hundreds of them.

My passenger is already belted in. I'm not. I was preparing to give him his next shot.

I launch toward my chair and buckle in before I have time to fully absorb the extent of my predicament.

"Incoming meteors," my female AI announces. "Approximately 516 of them."

"Take evasive maneuvers," I say. When I fully absorb what I'm seeing, though, I turn off autopilot and take over manual controls. There's no way to avoid a strike, the meteors are too dense. I don't even have time to shout commands or plan my next hop, I just hit the hyperdrive button and pray for the best.

One of the meteors bashes our hull as we pulse into hyperdrive. I'm a decent pilot, knowing enough to navigate and get myself from point A to point B. I have no idea what to do to recover from hull damage.

When we ease out of hyperdrive, we're wobbling. Five red lights are flashing on the dash, and my fuel gauge indicates empty even as the AI announces it over the speakers. I had the AI programmed to sound like it had some emotion instead of the mechanical monotone it originally had, but now that the voice sounds panicked, I'm regretting my decision. It seems counterproductive.

There's an asteroid visible on the screen. If I'm lucky, we can limp there with the limited amount of fuel in the lines. Luckily, the cabin's airtight hull wasn't pierced, or we'd both be dead by now.

Although I've never had the closest relationship with the man or woman upstairs, the back of my mind is trying to make last-minute introductions as the front of my mind is figuring how to get us to the asteroid spinning in the middle of my nav screen.

I have the presence of mind to launch the SOS space buoy as we hurtle toward land. Thantose teased me when I had the *Serenity* equipped with old-fashioned parachutes to slow the fall in case something like this happened. He told me I was wasting credits, informing me the chances were a million to one that I'd crash land.

*Take that, Captain Thantose. See? The parachutes deployed.* Now let's see if they'll keep my ass alive.

Not only do the parachutes slow our rapid descent once we hit atmo, but we get some additional help from trees and branches, thereby ensuring the vessel won't be salvageable once we hit soil.

And we do hit soil. The operative word being hit. Hard.

My AI reports in a calm, "welcome to this asteroid" sing-song tone, that the air is breathable, and the outside temperature is a humid eighty-two degrees Fahrenheit.

After scrambling out of the *Serenity* the moment I remove my seatbelt, I check to see if we're on fire, but luckily, no flames. Just one scraped, blackened, dysfunctional ship. I know nothing about where we are, what perils are around the next corner, or what will come next. After only the swiftest glance I know one thing, though—this vessel will not be flying off this rock. Ever.

My mind is racing with a million things I need to do in the next three minutes. I have to gather everything we might need to keep ourselves safe on this asteroid, then figure out what to do with sleeping beauty.

Weapons and ammo first. After climbing back into the ship, I toss them onto the mattress. Next, I throw food and water onto the bed.

The Dacian statue is in pieces. I guess ruining my sterling reputation as a pirate who gets the job done is the least of my concerns right now. Naomi, if I ever see her again, will just have to deal with it.

I had been about to administer an injection to So'Lan when we hit that meteor field. It went flying and I don't have the time or inclination to scrounge for it. The lion-man's days of lying comatose are over. If he doesn't come back to the land of the living soon, I'll be leaving without him.

150,000 credits sounded like a lot for a two-day trip. Now that I've got to keep the sorry sack of shit alive in a hostile environment, it's obvious those fuckers didn't pay me enough.

"So'Lan!" I say as I jiggle his shoulder. "So'Lan!"

He's going to wake up solidly in the middle of withdrawals and he's going to be pissed. Lucky me, he's not only a gladiator, but he's the proud owner of four-inch-long fangs—uppers *and* lowers. Yeah, I'm a little obsessed with those deadly looking fangs, and now I know he's also equipped with long, sharp claws.

Maybe I should leave him here to deal with shit on his own.

No. I may be cynical, but I'm not ready to administer a death sentence yet. I'll have to wake him up.

As we were plunging to what I was praying wasn't our fiery death, I saw some specs on the nav screen. The diameter of the asteroid is 311 miles. That's large as asteroids go, at least I think it is.

If I didn't know better, I'd think this was a planet. From what I see through the screen, it's lush, jungly. I've kicked around the galaxy enough that the orange, red, and yellow color palette isn't a complete shock.

"So'Lan. Bro. You've got two minutes to get your brain back online. After that, YOYO—you're on your own."

He's moaning now, thrashing his head from side to side. Trying to keep as far as I can from the business end of those teeth, I reach to use my thumbprint to release his cuffs.

As I'm about to back away, he grabs my wrists more swiftly than I would have thought possible for a male who just slept through a meteor shower and a crash landing on a hostile planet.

"What's happening?"

"You're on my vessel. We passed through a meteor storm on our way to Kryton. After I jumped to hyperdrive to save our asses, we crash-landed on this asteroid. I have no idea where we are. We're lucky to be alive. Actually, you're lucky I piloted us through it. So get your mitts off me and move your ass. We've got to get out of here before this ship blows."

I give him an angry, slit-eyed look, hoping he gets the message that I'm in charge and he can't order me around.

I'm not sure it works, but I see his eyes focus on me, then glance around the interior of the Serenity, and then notice the view of the jungle out the front screens. Understanding dawns on his face and motivates him to release his grip on my wrists and haul his ass out of bed.

"Your friend gathered some of your things. They're in a pack under your bed. Grab it and this," I hand him the pack with the food—I'm keeping the one with the weapons, "and meet me outside."

I've had enough experience with addicts to know he'll be of no help to me whatsoever. I step through the doorway and mentally say goodbye to the *Serenity*.

**So'Lan**

I'm disoriented. My skin is on fire. My thoughts are fuzzy, and it's taking an effort to stifle my urge to vomit. I'm not stupid, however, and it's obvious I'm in an emergency situation. Although I feel an *ince* from death, I know I need to leave. Fast.

I slip one pack over each shoulder, glance around to see if there's anything else left to salvage, then leap through the doorway.

The smell of fuel assaults my nose. I've been a gladiator all my adult life. I trained and sparred all day. I know nothing about spacecraft or engineering. I know the smell of combustible materials, though, and am smart enough to realize we'd better put as much distance as possible between us and the vessel.

My little human traveling companion is crashing through the forest. Even as I follow her, I wonder if she knows anything about stealth.

The area is thick with different species of trees. Most of them have rough, yellow bark and orange and crimson leaves. Where there aren't trees, the ground is covered with orange bushes.

If my mind was clear, I'd be calculating like a computer as I assess the thousand possible threats that could be assembling around us even as we stomp through the underbrush. I do know stomping isn't advised in any unknown situation.

"Ho!" I call to her. She doesn't act as if she even heard me. I don't know her name and don't want to shout. I think our crash and the sound of us thundering through the woods are enough to alert even the deafest of enemies to our location. Even so, I don't want to scream for the little Earther's attention.

After running to catch up with her, which, due to my nausea and lightheadedness, involved almost staggering into trees and tripping over an exposed root, I grab her upper arm.

"Ow!" she says in a whisper as she turns to me, gives me a fiery look, and yanks free of my grip.

"We need a plan," I say levelly.

"I have one. We're getting as far away from the crash site as possible, so when every wild beast in the forest investigates, we'll be long gone. Care to join me?" She tosses her head and seems about to walk away when she rubs the back of one finger under her nostrils, lifts one eyebrow, and says, "Ya got something there."

When my hand lifts in a similar gesture, I notice my nose is running.

"It's a symptom of withdrawal," she says smugly. "I imagine you're in the thick of it now."

With that, she marches forward.

Withdrawal. Right. I don't know how long I was on that ship, but it's obviously been a while since my last dose of pain medication. As sincerely as I argued with Dhoom in that meeting in his office, it was obvious he was right. I'm addicted to the Pethidrone I was using for pain. Who am I trying to fool? I like calling it by its medical name, but it's Synth. Everyone in the room knew it.

And, apparently, so does my traveling companion.

I'm sweating, nauseous, and agitated. And I'm on a strange planet with a female who obviously dislikes me. I want to yank her, stop her forward motion, and argue with her right here. I don't take orders from females, especially short, slight Earthers. I need to inform her of that, but I'll have to do that later. I don't have the energy right now.

She's a tiny thing, even for an Earther. I imagine a strong wind could blow her over. Her hair is almost white and is so short it barely reaches her neck. Walking around in her skin would be a vulnerable way to live. Perhaps that's why she dresses in black leather from the vest that covers a thin black skin-hugging shirt, to her pants, to her knee-high boots. I'll never tell her that her clothes do nothing to hide her small stature or womanly curves.

Again, I stride to catch up to her. As soon as I reach her, before I can tell her what our next move should be, she says, "The way I see it, we need to do two things. Since the foliage is too thick and I can't see the position of the sun, I have no idea what time of day it is. Before we lose daylight, we need to find a water source and somewhere to bed down where we'll have some modicum of protection."

I've been around the Earthers in the Sanctuary compound enough to know they seem to have left their primitive skills far behind in their evolutionary cycle. They long ago lost their abilities to scent other beings or sense danger. They lost any natural protection, like claws or fangs.

I hate to admit it, but she's right.

I sniff in through my nose, and despite the withdrawal-induced runny nose, I smell water to the right.

Striking off on my own, it's only after I've started forging a path toward the water that I call to her. Now I'm in the lead.

## Phoenix

Asshole. Why is it I've yet to meet a male of any species who isn't one?

Granted, he's more than a head taller than me, his stride is twice mine, and he could probably bench press five of me with one hand tied behind his back. It's just that he felt compelled to get the upper hand.

"Water is this way," he says, then sniffs.

That's going to get on my nerves soon. No, strike that. It's already on my nerves.

It only takes a few minutes for him to prove himself right. I hear running water. Soon, I see a meandering stream through the burnt-orange bushes.

We walk parallel to it for a while, as I wonder how we'll know if it's potable. He slows to walk next to me, then asks, "What's your name?"

"Phoenix."

"Tell me again how we got here."

I fill him in. It doesn't take long. "We were in a meteor storm," pretty much describes it. Perhaps by my tone of voice, I make it clear I'm not a fan of addicts, Synth or otherwise.

"Did they give you any Synth? For my breakthrough symptoms?" he asks, his eager voice bordering on desperate.

Oh no, he didn't. Is he considering returning to the crash site to rummage for drugs? Wow! He's got it bad.

"No, just a sedative to keep you out of it until we got to the facility on Kryton."

"Pherutan told me the symptoms of withdrawal. I didn't want to admit that I was addicted. I can no longer deny the truth. I have every symptom he listed. It's not going to be easy. I can feel my temper flaring every time a bug buzzes too near my head or a thorny bush snags my clothes. I'm trying to keep it under control."

I can't say this is the biggest shock of the day. I think the meteor storm and subsequent crash on an unknown chunk of rock win the prize, but I'll admit, his humble admission surprises me.

"Think the water's safe to drink?" I ask. We've got water in our packs, but I'd like to hoard it. There might be a time we really need it.

"Smells safe," he says, "but my nose is so busy running I'm not sure I trust it."

He makes his way through the underbrush, which is even thicker here, then squats at the water's edge. He doesn't reach to get a handful of water like I would. No, he dips his head down like an animal.

Although it's surprising to watch, I must admit it's interesting. When I encountered him on the floor of Dhoom's office, he'd been wearing nothing but a loincloth. It seemed to be the uniform of choice. That was how all the males dressed.

When I climbed onto the *Serenity*, I noticed someone had pulled some cargo pants on him. Perhaps it was out of deference to me, so I didn't have to be trapped in my vessel with a barely dressed male.

Watching him now, I take his inventory: broad back, wide shoulders, thick mane, well-defined abs. Although he's covered in short fur, I can see every muscle and sinew as it moves when he leans forward toward the water.

Although his ass is covered in black cargo pants which have a slit in it for his tail, I can see the nice, meaty globes pressing against the fabric as he moves. His tail is flicking side to side. I don't know whether that's due to his exposed position, or if it's just a symptom of withdrawal.

I have to force my eyes away from the sight so I can keep a lookout for predators. My hand is on the butt of the gun holstered at my hip. It felt like the Old West when I had the holster commissioned a few years back, but I've worn it more than once on some of the lawless planets I've visited.

"Smells okay," he says, then cups his hands to drink. So, he wasn't lapping at the water like a lion on the savannas of Africa. Oh well, it was nice to watch.

Oh shit! Is that what I think it is? Every muscle in my body goes on lockdown when I look closer.

"So'Lan! Run!" I don't know whether they're crocodiles or alligators, but they look just as prehistoric—and deadly—as the ones on Earth. Their bodies are at least ten feet long, nose to tail. They're green and powerful, and their jaws look as dangerous, albeit longer and narrower, than anything I've seen on Earth. The better to eat you with, my dear.

So'Lan stands and jumps backward in one lithe movement, but the reptiles are swiftly following him back onto dry land, their jaws snapping as they approach him.

I do the quickest 180 in the history of the world, checking out if anything is advancing from the rear. Nothing is coming from behind, but the enemy is approaching us from the water, which is now churning with them.

In another life, back on Earth, my folks took us to some alligator park in Florida on our way to Disney. There were hundreds, maybe thousands, of alligators in the water, all converging for feeding time when they tossed whole chickens into the water. The gator lucky enough to reach it first would swallow the bird in one gulp.

At the park, I was safely behind a chainlink fence as I watched the water roil with their writhing bodies as they fought for choice morsels with only one thought in mind—food. Right now? Nothing is separating me from their deadly jaws. At a quick glance, I'd say there are more than fifty, maybe a hundred of them.

So'Lan is already at my side. As I pull my weapon and aim, he says, "No!" and lifts me as if I weigh nothing.

"Hold on to my pants," he says. His voice has lost all semblance of humanity and comes out as a growl.

After tossing me over his shoulder, he runs with me into the woods and, without breaking his stride, climbs a tree.

As he uses all four limbs to climb, I tuck my cheek against his backside, throw my arms around his waist, try to avoid his heavy packs as they jostle against me, try to keep mine from falling off, and hold on for dear life. It takes a moment to register, but his tail has wrapped around me, trying to keep me from falling.

I have no idea how high he's climbed. My field of vision consists only of his golden fur. I just try not to fall as he keeps moving higher.

At last, he stops and eases me from his shoulder, then sets me on a branch.

Holy shit! We've got to be over two stories in the air, maybe higher. He's squatting near the tree trunk. I'm out on a limb. No wonder "out on a limb" is a cliché for being exposed and in danger. It sure feels that way.

My heart, instead of slowing now that we're supposedly out of danger, speeds up. I'm clutching the crimson bark beneath my fingers, but I'm terrified I'll fall off in a stiff wind.

One good thing. Although there are maybe thirty crockagators circling the tree, none of them have taken flight or started climbing after us. Good to know they can't fly or climb like monkeys. I think we're safe from them as long as we stay up here.

"We're safe up here," he says, his voice still rough.

"That's easy for you to say." I could swear this branch is swaying. I clutch it tighter, but unlike a certain someone who's sitting next to me, I don't have claws to help me hold on.

He looks at me as if for the first time. I imagine he's crawled out of his self-absorption for the first time since he woke from his sedative-induced stupor.

"You're afraid?"

"Unlike you, I don't have catlike reflexes."

He gives me an approximation of a smile, which flashes a bit of fang and makes his nose squinch in a move that reminds me of a human smelling something terrible. This makes me laugh.

"I imagine this isn't your best day," he says with a touch of warm compassion in his voice.

"No. I guess it's not yours either."

"I've had worse." His scant smile disappears.

I've been abducted by aliens and forced into sex work. But I have to admit, this is definitely my worst day. It makes me wonder what could be worse than this, but I shake my head to get that thought out of my head. That's something I don't want to imagine.

"Want to change places?" he offers.

"Yes."

He lithely stands, jumps high enough to grab the branch above our heads, and says, "Scoot over so you can hold onto the trunk."

Once he gracefully lands back on the branch and is sitting next to me again, we both peer over to check our friends on the ground. They look up, a few of them snapping their jaws loud enough we hear them from up here.

"I don't think they're going anywhere soon," he says. "I think we ought to spend the night here."

"Are you insane?" I can't help it. Those snarky words just leaped out of my mouth.

I hadn't noticed, but now that we're up higher, I can see the sun is setting. We're going to have to sleep somewhere, and the forest floor doesn't seem to be an option. But still…

"See that tree there?" He points through a few trees to one that has blue leaves mixed with crimson. The leaves are heart-shaped rather than oval. It's a different species than the one we're in. "See how thick some branches are where they meet the trunk? I'll go over and rig us a place to sleep."

I'm about to ask how he plans to "go over," but my mouth snaps shut as loudly as the crockagators when he Tarzans from tree to tree before I can get my criticism out of my mouth.

I wish I had a remote control, because I would sure as shit be hitting the rewind button to watch that over and over. He may be irritating and entitled, but seeing him go hand over hand as if he were part monkey as well as lion definitely caught my attention.

He's actually such a treat to watch I almost forget about the flock of gators down below. I'm caught up in his sheer economy of motion as he grabs some scarlet vines and begins weaving a mat.

Half an hour later, as the sun is about to dip below the horizon, he's finished his third mat and is tucking them against the crotch of the tree. Speaking of crotches, I guess his friends just tugged those cargo pants over his loincloth when they brought him aboard the *Serenity*, because he's removed his pants. Now it's just my furred, feline friend and his loincloth. His *bulging* loincloth.

He glances over at me for the first time since he left, then returns the way he came. While he was gone, I'd wondered how I was going to get from point A to point B, but it doesn't come as a surprise when he jumps onto a nearby branch and urges, "Leave your packs here, I'll come back for them. Climb onto my back."

I want to protest, to throw a hissy fit, to shake my head and refuse, but the alternatives are worse. If I fall asleep here, I'll fall to the ground the moment I reach REM sleep, and I can't even imagine how I would be able to swing by vines on my own.

"Piggyback it is," I say with a resigned shrug.

He reaches over, pulls me near him, and manages to help me onto his back. "Hold your forearms," he says after I've draped my arms under his chin. "Don't look down. Don't wiggle. And don't scream."

Shit. Did he have to remind me not to look down? Sure as shit, I'll mess up and do that first thing.

But I don't. I close my eyes and pay attention to So'Lan. His velvety fur under my chin, his warmth, and the iron muscles sliding underneath me as he goes hand over hand to our destination.

I keep my eyes tightly shut when we stop moving and don't open them until he clears his throat and says, "You can open your eyes."

The width of the new branch is surprising. From a distance, it didn't look much wider or sturdier than the one I was sitting on. Now that I'm here, I'd say it's at least a yard wide. He's braided a thick mat for us to rest on and made two woven blankets.

"Where did you learn to braid and weave?" They're impressive, but I don't want to tell him that.

"The youngest members of the training school were taught trades or crafts that were sold at the local markets to make credits to keep us fed and clothed until we were old enough to earn credits in the arenas," he explains as he hands one of the vine blankets to me.

"I'll be back," he says without a trace of awareness that he stole Arnie's line from the *Terminator*.

He retrieves my packs and is back in a few minutes. After handing them to me, he lies down, settles his cheek on his bicep, and gasps to catch his breath, his tongue lolling out the side of his mouth. Now that I pay attention, I notice his breathing is labored, and his nose is acting up again.

"You okay?"

"I get the feeling you don't want to hear about my escalating detox symptoms. Suffice it to say, I'm pushing through it."

A moment later, he lurches to his feet, doesn't take the time to grab a hanging vine, just leaps to a nearby tree and then the next, then settles to his knees and retches over the side.

I avert my eyes partly because I don't want to intrude on what, to anyone, should be a private moment. I also have no desire to watch. But it's hard to ignore, especially when it goes from regular vomiting to dry heaves. It sounds rough.

When he finally stops for a while, I glance over. His shoulders are hunched and he's panting.

"I have water in my pack!" I call. I imagine it would taste good right about now.

He stands with effort, seems to gather his energy, and returns, almost missing his handhold on the last vine. It's a long way down, and he would be greeted by some unfriendlies when he gets there. I'm glad he made it.

He tries to ration the water, but he keeps sipping and shivering and sipping some more. When he settles on his side of the mat, I say, "I guess we should come up with a plan?"

"Step one, don't fall out of the tree in your sleep," he says, his voice husky from all that retching.

"And? Step two?" I'm interested in what his thoughts are.

"Don't get killed by predators."

"And?" Is he playing coy?

"I lived in a gladiator training school, a *ludus*, all my adult life until my master, Daneur Khour threw me into an underground dungeon. I don't have experience surviving in a jungle or being pursued by wild animals. And it's not just the animals I worry about. I'm thinking this may be an asteroid, but it's got a lot going for it. Drinkable water, breathable air, food. I'm more concerned about inhabitants of the humanoid variety than those hungry reptiles below us."

As if on cue, one of them snaps his jaws.

Now *I* feel like hurling. I hadn't given that more than a passing thought. There's a good chance this planet is inhabited? We've got weapons, but just how long would they last against a tribe? Speaking of which, "Why didn't you want me to use my weapon against those beasts down there?"

"Just as I said, I wonder if there are humanoids on this planet. Until we figure it out, I don't want to announce our presence."

I nod. I have to admit, he was ahead of me on that. I couldn't think past finding water and shelter. Then the shock of seeing the crockagators had me grabbing my weapon in a blind panic.

"I wasn't thinking clearly after the crash," he admits. "You got a better look at the crash site than me. So you think there's any chance…?"

I shake my head. "We can circle back if you want, but I don't think we're flying out of here on that. Damaged by the meteor strike, then obliterated by the crash, and to top it off, we rode in on fumes. We're out of fuel. So, no. I think that ship has sailed. We might get rescued, though. I sent out an emergency buoy." I give him a falsely optimistic shrug.

"What do you think our chances of rescue are?"

Wow, he looks so hopeful, eyebrows raised in expectation. I hate to tell him there's no Santa Clause, but I answer, "Slim. To be honest? None." I hate to dash his hopes, but I've found realism is better than false hope.

So'Lan lies down in a tight ball and makes a sound between a purr and a moan.

"How are you doing?"

"Don't ask if you don't want to know. I get the distinct impression you've been judging me since you met me."

Busted. I have been.

"I'm intimately acquainted with the issue of addiction. So, yeah, I suffer from compassion fatigue."

"Then to answer your question, I'm doing well. Great, actually," he says. He lies there, his eyes fluttering, and then he makes that pathetic moan again.

"Hungry?" I ask. I know he just hurled, but it would be impolite to eat without offering him half of my stash.

My question elicits an ungrateful grunt.

"I'll take that as a no," I say, then unwrap a nutrition bar and try to eat as quietly as possible.

When I'm done eating, it's pitch black and So'Lan is fast asleep. I might as well get some shuteye. Unless we find a Hilton around the next bend, tomorrow's going to be a long day.

There aren't many options for sleeping positions. It's So'Lan and me on a surface narrower than a twin bed. I nestle my back to his front, and even in his restless sleep, he accommodates me. I had worried I'd roll off the platform in my sleep, so I don't complain when, a minute later, he slings his heavy arm around my waist.

After the day I've had, you'd think I would already have dropped into a deep sleep, but I'm wide awake.

I'm on another planet, well, an asteroid. We've already established it's unfriendly territory. Possible humanoids or not, if those crockagators are still waiting for us in the morning, we're going to have to use our lasers.

My mind keeps circling from one worry to another. Finally, to break the cycle, I try to focus on something else. What do you know? I have just the thing.

There's a warm arm around my waist, tugging me close. His furred chest is plastered to my back.

I thought my eyes had flickered closed, but they must be open, because I watch as his tail lifts above me, then curls around my hip.

"Did you do that on purpose?" I whisper.

The only response I get is the sound of snapping jaws drifting to me through the quiet night air.

I have to admit, him tucking me close gives me a sense of security. Even though it's a false sense of security, I'm not about to argue.

When we were on the vessel, I tried not to think about him at all. He was just cargo. But try as I might, I did think about him. And not one of those thoughts was flattering. Well, except for admiring his obvious physical attributes.

I have no use for addicts. I may not be the smartest person in the galaxy, but I am capable of learning from my mistakes. Addicts are bad news and I want to stay as far from them as possible.

I have to admit, though, So'Lan has been a pretty good traveling companion. Let's be honest, he saved my life back there. Even if I'd used my weapon, the odds weren't great that I would have escaped alive because there were so many of those critters. I never would have been able to climb this tree on my own.

He has fur to keep him warm. He made the two blankets for me.

"Why are you making it so hard to hate you?" I whisper into the dark.

# Chapter Three

**P**hoenix

I must have fallen asleep, but I'm pulled back to reality in a hurry. At first, my foggy brain has to remember I crash-landed and am on an asteroid. Then it thinks there's an earthquake, which isn't precise, because we're not on Earth. Then I realize it's So'Lan who's shaking like a leaf. His body is so bulky, it's making the thick branch tremor.

If I don't do something, he's shivering so wildly he's going to fall. It's a long way down. His teeth are chattering, and by teeth, I mean those humongous fangs are snapping together as loudly as the reptiles down below.

I recall my aunt telling me that when her husband had a bone marrow transplant, one of the meds they gave him caused this type of reaction. She said no nurses were around and right after she pushed the call button, she threw herself on top of him to give him her body warmth. My uncle would always nod at this point and say, "Yep. She saved my life."

Although this situation is far different from that, the primary reason being the aforementioned four-inch fangs, I roll on top of him. I'm bowed up, carefully keeping my carotid out of striking distance of those teeth.

"So'Lan!" I say, then repeat his name, louder.

He opens his eyes, which are bleary and unfocused.

"So'Lan, I think this is your withdrawal."

He grunts in agreement, then lays his head on the mat, too debilitated to lift it.

"Promise you won't bite me? I'll keep you warm."

"Promise," he whispers through parched lips.

I'm riding him like a bucking bronc. It's a miracle either of us can stay on the limb, which is not only narrow, but still trembling like it's in the eye of a hurricane.

"Talk to me," he urges. His eyes are closed and his lips are stretched into a snarl. I think that's his way of keeping his teeth hidden. Good move.

"What?"

"Talk."

I guess he wants something to hold on to as he rides this out. I can see the shaking and the runny nose. I wonder what other symptoms he has coursing through the rest of his body.

One thing is certain. He's in pain.

I can't pay too much attention to the words spilling from my lips. I'm far more worried about keeping us both on this branch. I have no idea what to say, so I start narrating the plot from one of my favorite shows.

"You," he says, then goes into such a violent paroxysm I wonder if it's a seizure.

"You want to hear about me?" I ask when his tremors slow.

"Mmm."

"Let's see. Born in South Dakota. Not much of note up there on the windswept plains. My town was known for having the world's biggest buffalo. That's like a big *anlak*. It wasn't very exciting. It wasn't real. It was fabricated. It was maybe five times as tall as you."

I cast my mind to try to think of anything else to tell him that isn't personal.

"It's cold there. Winters are long. Brutal might be a better description."

"Mmm." I think my words are giving him something to pay attention to other than his misery. His "mmm" is his way of asking me to continue.

"I was an average student. I kinda had trouble paying attention. Several teachers suggested I had ADD. It's a disorder that makes it hard to pay attention, but my dad didn't want to believe that so I didn't get any meds for it."

He settled for a moment, but now he's shivering again. He's in misery, that's for sure. I don't know what possesses me, but I change my center of gravity to keep an even lower profile against him so I can graze his cheek with my palm.

He's hot, his fur is damp. It's warm out here in the jungle, but his body is warmer than that.

"We're going to get you through this, So'Lan," I say as I pet his cheek.

His blue eyes pop open with a pleading look.

"So'Sad, So'Lan," I say, trying to commiserate with him.

It's clear my talking is helping, so I come up with something else to say. "I had a pretty uneventful life until slavers abducted me. Actually, it's a pretty good business model. You know, low cost of goods, high rate of return. Brilliant, really, since the Feds turn a blind eye to human trafficking."

His body has settled. I think the poor guy has fallen back to sleep. When I roll off him, though, his limbs start quivering again. I climb back on and lie against his chest. It seems as long as I don't move, he'll sleep peacefully.

I hear his rapid heartbeat. That doesn't sound healthy. It doesn't even seem safe. It's racing far too fast. I pat his cheek and murmur into his ear, "You're going to live through this. I know from experience. You might be better as soon as the sun comes up."

I pet him until his heart slows and his body quits shuddering. When I get ready to roll off him, though, I realize his muscular arms are encircling me and his tail is wrapped around my ankle. I guess I'm not going anywhere.

How can my body morph from red alert in caretaking mode to aroused? But that's what happens. I haven't felt this in a while. My nipples are pricked as they drag against his strong pecs. More insistent, though, is the drumbeat between my legs.

It's not hard to understand. In order to keep us from falling off the branch, I'm straddling him. My knees are cushioned from the rough bark by the mat he made, but this position has my clit rubbing on his cock.

When I was on high alert, I didn't even notice my precarious posture. Now I can't ignore it.

He's not human, not even particularly humanoid. But he's handsome in that dangerous way I've always found attractive. I'm nothing if not consistent. And my penchant for bad boys has gotten me into trouble in the past.

The moment it's safe, I'm going to get as far away from him as I can on this narrow branch. In the meantime, his arms surround me more tightly, and he hitches me closer to his head. The position is less blatantly sexual, but no less dangerous. Now we're clearly cuddling.

After nestling his chin against the top of my head, the deep rumble of a purr vibrates through his chest. It's so… reassuring. How can I blame myself for melting into his embrace?

**So'Lan**

I've been dead inside for as long as I can remember. I was little more than a babe when slavers stole me. I remember nothing from that life. The harshness of gladiator schools is all I've ever known.

I'm driven. It's who I am. I wonder if I'd had parents who raised me to be an accountant or teacher if I would have been just as dedicated to my training. Probably. Set me a goal and I will meet, then exceed it.

I was on my way to becoming a Pinnacle gladiator until a series of events led to several losses in a row.

I've always been a self-contained unit, needing nothing from anyone. Which is good, because I discovered early in life that wanting and needing got me nowhere. But being thrown into that dungeon, starved, tied down while my fangs were brutally yanked out, with no hope of escape—broke me.

There's something about this little Earther. Cocky little thing. It's as if she doesn't know she should be two heads taller or be the owner of a cock instead of a *xyzca*. Look at her in her black leather outfit, a laser holster at her hip.

She has her secrets, just as I do. She wants me to think she's a hard one, but she smelled of fear all day. No, she reeks of it. She's terrified. The crash, those monsters at the foot of the tree, me. She pretends she's in control, but she's petrified.

Now that my teeth aren't chattering and my body is calming down, I can comfort her. She'd never listen to my words. She said it earlier when she thought I was asleep. She wants to hate me. But she allows my touch.

As dead as I am inside, my protective instincts are strong. I rearrange her so I'm cradling her on my chest, my arms shelter her. Unsheathing my claws, I comb through her short, golden hair. It's almost white. Blonde, the Earthers call it.

I comb her hair for a while until her body stands down and melts into me. Then I retract my claws and pet her head. She's feigning sleep and allowing my touch.

I seldom purr. It's an uncontrollable response that happens when I'm calm and happy—which is rare. It's as if my body didn't get the message that I've crash-landed on an unknown asteroid, am going through withdrawal hell, and am being stalked by wild beasts. I'm purring because of Phoenix.

**Phoenix**

I wake to a cacophony of noises as every bird in the forest feels compelled to greet the dawn with a squawk. Lifting one eyelid, I see the gray shades of dawn brighten the sky.

Shit. I'm lying next to So'Lan as if we're lovers. My bent leg is casually spread across his thigh, and my hand is curled on his chest, which is rumbling from his purrs. His fingers are tangled in my hair.

We've got a lot more to worry about than whatever the undercurrent is between us. I roll out of his embrace to peer over the side of the branch. I don't see any crockagators. That doesn't mean they haven't retreated five feet to hide under the bushes, though. The fact that I don't see them doesn't reassure me at all.

"We're going to need to find shelter today," I announce, knowing he has to be awake after all that bird noise.

"Yes. We need to scout, find shelter, and create a safe place," he says.

I nod.

"And you, So'Lan? I thought you were going to die last night. How are you doing? And yes, I really want to know."

"I think the worst is over. No shaking. No nausea."

"I hate to break it to you, but you might not be over it."

"If that's the case, I guess we should get to work." He stands and stretches, putting his hands on the small of his back as he leans backward. He emits a low, rumbling purr of enjoyment, then says, "I've been thinking about where we should go today. I vote we go deeper into the forest, looking for shelter. I keep remembering the smell of fuel at the crash site and don't think it will be safe to return to check it out."

"I agree," I say. I'd had that thought during one of the many times I awoke in the middle of the night to worry.

"Okay. Stay here, I'll be back."

Before I can question where he's planning to go, he leaps from branch to branch as he moves deeper into the forest. Watching his golden back, I hear signs of struggle, followed by shrieking. That couldn't be him, could it?

Panic rises as I wonder if he's hurt. How will I be able to help? The medbot is miles away in the *Serenity*, and So'Heavy has to weigh well over 300 pounds. I can't even imagine how I'll get down from this tree.

He returns to our tree, using only one hand to cling to the vines. In the other, he's clutching a huge handful of birds. By their lack of movement, I assume they're dead. Their thin, sticklike legs are clutched in his hand.

"I looked through the pack my comrades sent with me. Useless clothing. We'll leave it here. Since we're down to two packs, can you wear them both?" he asks.

I nod.

"Put them on," he urges. "As soon as I'm done, you're going to jump onto my back and we're going to climb down."

He heaves one bird at a time, flinging them all the way across the water. It's at least the length of a football field.

We take a moment to watch as first one crockagator, then the whole herd, scurry to the river, then swim across. We pause long enough to watch as the ground on the other side of the river turns green because there are so many of them. We hear them roar in anger and snap at each other as they fight each other for the birds.

"I hope they all went across the river for the buffet," he says as he crouches for me to climb onto his back.

The trip to the ground isn't nearly as terrifying as it was going up. It feels great to be on land again, although I'm going to keep my eyes peeled for more of those deadly critters.

As soon as we're on land, we strike off at a jog into the depths of the forest.

Keeping my hand near the butt of my weapon, I allow myself to enjoy the beauty of this place. In my meager experience, asteroids are dusty affairs, devoid of most native life. Perhaps this was terraformed at one time. That might not bode well for us, since terraforming means humanoids. Call me cynical, but humanoids usually don't treat interlopers well.

We see numerous bird species and little chipmunky things that are not only cute, but gorgeous because they're striped blue and scarlet.

Although I don't see any, the occasional screeching we hear sounds like monkeys. That's just my imagination, though, because it's just a guess what alien animal could make such a sound.

So'Lan and I stop only long enough for brief sips of water before we hurry on our way again. We each eat an energy bar as we walk.

"How are your symptoms?" I ask after we've traveled for a few hours.

"Better. I know how to fight through hell. I did it on the sands of the arena. I managed during three *annums* in that underground hellhole. I will do it now."

We keep moving. The farther we go, the less I believe we'll ever return to the *Serenity*. I have to admit I was holding out hope that someday we'd go back there and fly off this rock. But I let that wish go.

After the sun reaches its apex and it's after noon, I allow myself the slightest moment to mourn. I released that emergency buoy, but I'm not sure if it was able to get through the atmosphere and into space, or, even if it deployed, if anyone will find it.

My eyes fill with tears when I admit to myself that So'Lan and I might not find a way off this rock. The odds aren't looking good.

When we encounter a huge tree like the one we slept in last night, we both stop in our tracks. The trunk is wide, wider than almost anything we've seen.

It's not the size of the tree that catches our attention, though. There, about ten feet off the ground, is a carving. We're silent, and for a moment it feels as if the entire forest has quieted to underscore our thunderous discovery.

It's a head-to-toe carving of a male. A male who looks exactly like So'Lan. Powerful humanoid body, feline face, terrifying fangs, lion-like mane. He's carrying what looks to me like a laser rifle. There are rays coming out of his head, similar to some I've seen in Renaissance paintings.

"Wow," I whisper.

So'Lan is standing tall, still as a statue.

"Melodie said your species is Ton'arr. Were your people big on conquering other peoples? Other planets?"

"I was abducted at a young age. I know nothing about my people other than what I've read after my release from the dungeon over the last few *lunars*."

"I think we just confirmed there are intelligent life forms on our little asteroid," I say, finally tearing my gaze from the carving and pegging my gaze on So'Lan.

"Aye. Perhaps my people?"

I nod, my mind flying with questions about whether this new little factoid makes us more safe, or less.

"Look!" I point through the trees. There are bluffs maybe a mile ahead. Bluffs might mean caves. Caves mean shelter.

*Maybe,* my rational mind reminds me. *Caves might mean shelter. Caves might mean vicious animals. Caves might mean other humanoids. Enemies might live in caves.*

I refuse to argue with myself. After our run-in with the crockagators, we've got to find a place to bed down for the night.

"Should we try to reach the bluffs?" he asks.

I have to admit, I appreciate he doesn't pretend he has all the answers. As he's quick to point out, he's never been in an alien jungle before. Rather than acting as if he knows it all, he's checking it out with me.

"Wild animals could be hiding there, or angry humanoids," I give voice to my fears. "But it sounds like our best option if we don't want to sleep in a tree again tonight."

My mind flashes to last night's sleeping arrangements. There were moments when it felt comfortable that his arms—and tail—were wrapped safely around me. His fur was so soft and warm, I allowed myself to enjoy the moment. I guess sleeping in a tree again tonight wouldn't be the worst thing in the world.

We strike off toward the bluffs. As we get closer, our prospects seem to be looking up. They're covered in the same vines my friend Tarzan was swinging on last night. There are some dark shadows that hint we might find some caves inside the rock. This might turn out well, providing they aren't occupied.

The bluffs were farther away than they appeared. I hope we get there with enough daylight to explore and set up camp.

My body reacts before my mind engages. It doesn't take me more than a second to put a label on the sound drifting to my ears. Drums!

I suck in a rasping breath as every muscle in my body tenses.

"Shit!" I whisper.

Drums mean people. Primitive people. Maybe I've seen too many movies, but I'm not imagining a welcome party.

"What direction are the drums coming from?" I ask, my eyes wide in fear.

He may not know his way around a jungle, but his hearing is better than mine. His rounded feline ears swivel, then he points to our right.

"Should we keep heading for the bluffs? I think we should turn around and sleep in another tree tonight."

"I agree," he says.

We both turn around, take a few steps, and all of a sudden I'm alone in the forest. So'Lan is gone.

He's snarling from above, caught in a net made of vines.

"Shit!"

At least I have a knife. I always keep one in my boot. You never know when you might need one. But he's high above me, maybe twenty feet.

"I'll be right there," I tell him confidently, even as inside my head I wonder how I'm going to reach him.

This was a trap, like you see in the movies. Someone made this net, camouflaged it, and at some point is going to come retrieve their prey. I need to hurry.

I can't quite figure out how I'm going to climb high enough to cut the vines. I think it will be quicker to toss him my knife, but almost immediately realize that won't work. It's a bladed knife in a sheath built into my boot. I'd have to toss it up, possibly slicing him in the process. For a moment I flash on a picture of him using his teeth or claws to cut through the thick weave, but the knife is his quickest path to freedom.

"Can you slide your hand through the netting?"

"I'm pretty sure."

"Good. Can you shimmy out of your pants? Use them to protect your hand? Then I'll toss the knife to you and you can cut your way out."

He's working his way out of his pants, the net jiggling in midair as he struggles to do it. I'm feeling like the galaxy's most brilliant inhabitant. I figured out a way to free him that didn't involve me falling out of a tree.

He suddenly quits moving. I can't see his face, but there's something about his posture that screams danger.

Before I have time to turn around and investigate, I'm surrounded by spear-waving natives.

They're tall, maybe So'Lan's height, maybe less. They're not built like him, though. They're thin and lithe and well-armed. Emphasis on the well-armed part. This is clearly a hunting party.

My chest is heaving in fear as I try to catch my breath. I drop the knife, raise my hands in the universal position for "I give up" and turn slowly, assessing my situation as I see the extent of our predicament.

There are six of them. Five males and a female. Their skin is light green, like new-growth leaves in spring. It would be pretty if the people wearing the skin weren't looking at me like I'm their next meal.

Their faces have thick plating on their foreheads, with ridged bumps along their brows and circling under their eyes. Their emerald-green eyes are burning with excitement—or maybe anger. Whatever their emotion, it's not friendly.

I'm wondering if they want to kill me and then eat me, or just eat me. I guess it really doesn't matter.

They're chattering among themselves. Their language is incomprehensible. If I live long enough, my upgraded, self-learning translator will interpret their language. In the meantime, I'm clueless.

I consider using the laser pistol at my hip, but that would be futile. Six against one isn't great odds, even though it's my laser against their spears. The fact is, all six spears are inches from me. I'd be dead before I unholster my weapon.

The one saving grace in all of this is that none of them have looked up. Maybe they stumbled upon me and have no idea their trap has been sprung. If So'Lan can just stay quiet up there, they might do whatever they're going to do to me and then be on their way. With fangs like his, he'll chew his way out of the trap long before he starves to death.

My translator is worth the jaw-dropping price I paid. It's already telling me a few words in English. Unfortunately, it only has nouns and pronouns so far. I hear "she," and then "spear." My heart squeezes in my chest when I hear the word "kill."

Shit. Not good. My mouth is dry and I'm so scared I'd be running into the forest if there weren't spear tips an inch from my skin in every direction.

Perhaps So'Lan has an upgraded translator, too. Well, of course he does. The folks at Sanctuary seemed to be loaded. I mean really, giving me 150,000 credits to deliver him on a two-day trip? That was a stupid amount of money.

The moment these people say the word "kill," though, he roars. Once, twice, then he struggles against his bonds.

The arguing around me ceases, the spears are removed from around my body, and as if they practiced, they all drop to one knee, heads bowed in respect. No. It's bigger than respect. It's awe.

# Chapter Four

**S**o'Lan

I've spent my entire life taking care of myself. I had to. No one else was going to do it. From a young age, I was in the care of people who didn't care. I was a commodity. My life was expendable.

Not only did the people in charge of me as a youngling have no concern for me or my welfare, but the males I trained with kept their distance, too. We all learned early that we can't get too attached to other gladiators. Who wants to risk getting close to someone you might have to fight or kill the next day?

My history with females? I was a good fighter, on track to becoming a Pinnacle. I've had many. One after every win in the arena. I've never been tempted to bond with any. They were paid for by the *hoara*, and usually entered my cell already reeking of other males.

Until we were rescued and created Sanctuary, I've been alone my entire life. And that's been fine with me.

I've only known the little Earther for a day, but when I saw those savages surround her, point their *dracking* weapons at her, touch her with the points of their spears, I wanted to kill them without benefit of my sword. I wanted to tear them apart with my claws and fangs.

Even though I'm bound in this tight netting, my tail is flicking in fury. I can barely keep myself from roaring while they argue about her fate. I only keep myself quiet because if they don't discover me, I'll be able to tear my way out of this trap and follow her. I'll be able to find and free her.

When my translator speaks the word "kill" in my ear, I can't control the roar that bellows from deep in my throat.

I shutter my lids in self-loathing for a moment, hating myself for giving away my presence. My stealth, staying hidden, was the only way I would have half a chance to rescue her.

When I open my eyes, I fully expect to see them cocking their wrists, ready to hurl their spears at me. Instead, they are each kneeling on one knee, heads bowed in obeisance.

One stands, climbs the tree as if he were born to do it, and cuts me loose. All the while, he is jabbering. My translator may not have learned much of his language, but his body and the tone of his voice speak volumes.

He's speaking an apology. He repeats it over and over. Sometimes the words are exactly the same, sometimes there are variations, but he is abjectly sorry.

After he cuts a slit in the bottom of the net, I easily drop to the forest floor.

Five of the six of them form a perfect line in front of me, drop farther to the ground so their chests scrape it, their arms in front of them. All of them join in a song. Although the one still standing looks ashamed for doing so, he motions for me to remove my pack as he points his weapon at me.

I've never been to a temple. They didn't allow slaves to do such things. I was young when I was stolen. Some of my comrades came to the gladiator life at an older age. They had learned their parents' religion. At certain times of the year, they sang religious songs. That's what this sounds like.

I reach out to Phoenix, tug her to my side, and wrap my arm around her waist. Only one male is holding a spear, but I know deep in my bones that although they are giving me respect, if I attack him or try to leave, they won't allow it.

I'm going to have to stay for a while, and the only way to keep Phoenix safe is to make it clear she's important to me, that she's under my protection.

When their song is complete, my translator is performing at about 25%. They stand, and the one who climbed into the tree to release me bows from the waist and invites us to their village. The muscles in Phoenix's body tighten. I haven't known her long, but I can sense she's going to reject their offer and make a run for it.

I snug her closer and nod my head, agreeing to follow.

"They won't take no for an answer," I tell her softly after they surround us and head toward their village. "We need to figure out what's going on before we plan an escape. Where's your pistol?"

"They took the pack and grabbed my pistol when monkey-guy climbed that tree to set you loose. They even have my knife. What about you? I saw them take your pack."

"I've got nothing but my loincloth."

As we walk, the natives say nothing. They sneak glances at us from time to time in a way I imagine I would have looked at a traveling king if he had shown up at my *ludus*.

"I'll keep you safe, Phoenix. We will figure this out. I'll protect you."

**Phoenix**

So'Lan is going to keep me safe, huh? Twelve hours ago, he was barfing his guts out because he was detoxing from Synth. He shivered so hard he almost rolled off the branch and fell two stories to his death. Now Mr. Big Shot is somehow going to keep me safe from these natives?

And what's with the hero worship? They were flat on the ground in supplication to him a moment ago.

Ahhh. I think I understand.

"I think this has something to do with the tree carving," I tell him. My mind is flying with possibilities. Did his species visit here years ago? Help these people? Conquer them? One thing is clear. The natives think So'Lan is worth worshipping.

The female breaks off from the group and takes off at a run. I understood enough of their conversation to figure out she's going to tell the village of our arrival. Well, of So'Lan's arrival. Maybe they'll get busy cooking us a welcome feast. I can only hope the meal doesn't consist of human flesh—mine.

We arrive at a village consisting of round wooden buildings with roofs made of mud. There's a firepit at the center of the hub.

I'd bet money every single inhabitant of the village is watching our arrival. Although these people are primitive, they're advanced enough to have spears and knives as well as bows and arrows. They know how to weave. They're wearing colorful textile clothing.

Their green faces are filled with awe when we arrive. Many drop to the ground in a similar fashion to what we saw in the forest.

Two males are in front of the group. When they're introduced, my translator confirms what I'd already surmised. "This is Ammu, our high priest. I am Ba'Rell, the chief."

They are elders, not ancient, but if they were human, I'd put them at about fifty. The one with the most colorful feathers on his tall headpiece appears to be the shaman. The male with the fez-shaped headgear is the chief.

They stand paralyzed for a moment as they look us up and down. They're not really looking at me, actually, their eyes don't leave So'Lan. Their mouths have popped open in awe.

When the shaman doesn't immediately follow suit after the chief goes down on one knee, he receives a barked reprimand. These two are giving respect, but we're still being held at the point of six spears. Every male in the village also has a weapon in their hand or at their hip. So'Lan is being both revered and held hostage. Me? I'm just being held hostage.

"We have waited a long time," the chief says solemnly after he stands. "Some," he looks pointedly at the shaman by his side, "doubted your return. Me? I always knew you would come."

He throws his arms out wide. "Welcome to our village. We will place you in a fine hut, provide you sustenance after your long journey, and bring you water to wash off the dust. Give us time to prepare a feast and we will give you a fitting tribute this evening."

He bows, then gives orders to several tribesmen who run off to follow his commands.

"We have followed your instructions for generations and have always remained prepared for your return. Never fear. You will receive your homage as well as your tribute. Follow me."

He leads us to the largest hut, which is in the first circle of buildings around this common area. I notice the other dwellings' doors are made of colorful hanging fabric. This one is made of sticks and has a closure. I doubt it's to be locked from the inside. It seems we're honored prisoners.

"I will take your maidservant to other quarters. The virgins we keep at the ready awaiting your return can serve you from now forward."

He gestures to a cluster of young males with a dismissive wave of his hand, indicating they should take me away. There's a sneer on his face, as if I'm a piece of refuse he can't wait to dispose of.

So'Lan's arm is still tucked around me. Although we've both been on high alert this whole time, I feel his muscles tighten next to me. He gives a warning feline rumble when the males approach me.

"Mine!" To make his meaning even more clear, he turns us slowly, making certain to keep us hip to hip as we rotate in a complete circle. He stabs a hard stare at every male who has the balls to look at us. I imagine every species in the galaxy, no matter how wide the communication gap, would understand his message—hands off my female.

The chief nods once, then says, "I'm sorry to offend. Of course you wish to keep this servant at the ready for your needs until you meet your mate."

We're escorted into the hut, and I'm not surprised when two armed sentries take up posts outside our door.

There's a wide bed with a colorful blanket near the back of the windowless round structure. I don't know what the mattress is filled with, but it looks comfortable. There's a wooden table and two stumps for stools in the corner. Otherwise, the room is bare.

To my surprise, So'Lan falls heavily on the bed. He's been so strong today. He had no complaints as we walked. He even set our brutal pace and never lagged. I hadn't realized how much the strenuous journey took a toll on him.

"Still feeling the effects of withdrawal?"

"Aye."

There's a timid knock on the door, and So'Lan bolts upright and puts on an expression meant to intimidate. A teenage female, naked from the waist up, eyes focused on the ground, brings in a pitcher of water and a hollow wooden cup.

Another female, equally undressed, enters behind her. She has a wooden platter laden with exotic, colorful fruit, bread that looks like warm, thick tortillas, and a steaming bowl of something with a wooden spoon sticking out of it.

They set the food and drink on the table and then wait for instructions. They keep their heads bowed, and their hands in the prayer position folded between their breasts, which are thrust out for So'Lan's viewing pleasure.

I assumed he would dismiss them immediately. Instead, he asks questions in their language. How does he know their language?

"What do you want?"

They both drop to their knees and say, "To please you, my Lord."

"What do you expect?"

They look at each other, eyes wide in confusion as they try to second guess the correct answer. One of them finally gives a nervous laugh and answers, "To please you, Lord. To catch your eye so you will…" She looks at him directly for a split second, then returns her glance to the floor, swallows, and continues, "Choose to mate with me."

Both females are staring at the floor as if it was the most interesting thing in the world. My gaze darts to So'Lan. The only emotion he reveals is the slight flare of his nostrils. I don't know him well enough to interpret that.

"Leave," he says.

As soon as the door closes behind them, I go to the table and guzzle a cup of water, then bring him a full pottery cup. He's already lying down, panting from the effort of holding it together in front of those two girls.

"What the fuck?" I whisper as I hand him the drink. "How did you learn their language? My translator is picking up more and more of what they're saying, but I can't speak a word of their language."

"I grew up in *ludii* and moved every *annum*. They housed me with dozens of species. After a while, I realized I had a knack for languages. It comes naturally to me."

I shrug. I'd read somewhere that if exposed to other languages at a young age, the brain develops a facility for learning language. I guess he hit the jackpot.

I doubt they poisoned our food. If the tribe wanted us dead, that would have happened back in the forest. I pop a grape-like object into my mouth, carry the platter to the bed, set it next to So'Lan, then join him.

"We need to figure a way out of this," I say around a mouthful of fluffy, warm tortilla.

"Aye," he groans. "Give me a moment, then we'll talk."

He needs more than a moment. The next time I glance at him, he's fallen asleep.

After inhaling a few more bites of food, I lie back on the bed and inspect him. I've tried to hate him, to stay angry at him because of his Synth addiction and his shitty behavior in Dhoom's office. But Melodie explained he'd been at death's door. His owner must have abused him badly. It sounds like he really needed those pain meds, at least in the beginning.

I shrug. I understand how someone can get addicted to painkillers. It's recreational users I have a beef with. I promise myself I'm over it. I'm going to let go of my grudge. He's detoxing now. He's done nothing except protect me since we crashed. I vow to put all that behind me.

I stare at him. He's a handsome male. My fingers itch to stroke his fur. It was so warm and soft when he tugged me close last night.

I've had a thousand opportunities to see him from every angle as we walked today.

Several months ago, he may have been so debilitated he had to be carried out of the dungeon they rescued him from, but he's in fine shape now. And I do mean fine.

His ass, sadly covered in clothes until he was released from that net, filled out his pants in spectacular fashion. His chest, perfectly muscled, looks even sexier because it's covered in golden fur. His face, now that I'm used to its feline features, is an ideal combination of symmetry and danger. And those aquamarine-blue eyes? I could dive into them.

I fall back onto the mattress, then reach to touch his forearm, as if I need to maintain contact.

It took me months after my abduction to see anything appealing in any alien species. Well, *males* of any species. I was terrified, then bitter, then furious. Being sold for men's pleasure, no matter what they looked like, didn't endear them to me.

It was only after Gant took a shine to me and bought me that my feelings changed. I never grew to like him, and certainly never trusted him, but I tolerated him.

Can you blame me that I held a grudge all the years I was with him? He rented me by the hour every day for weeks before I wheedled my way into his plans. When he told me he needed a first mate on his pirate vessel, I recited my curriculum vitae to him.

I lied through my teeth, telling him I grew up on Nantucket. Not that he'd heard of it, of course. But I told him I'd been captaining seagoing vessels for years. Although I don't know a jib from a mainsail, I talked a good game.

Then I recited all of my navigating experience. Of which, if you got down to it, I had zero. But one thing I knew. I've always been smart. I knew if *he* was smart enough to captain a space vessel, *I* certainly could.

And I knew how greedy he was. Buy me once and have me work for him forever? And get free, endless pussy, too? Eventually, I wore him down and wound up on his ship.

He quickly realized I had no helpful skills, but by that time, I'd made myself invaluable by cooking for him, sucking and fucking whenever he wanted, and learning how to fly.

I was with Gant for years. It only took a few months to ignore the fact that he was butt ugly. I hated his mottled gray skin and the knobs on his face and head. Eventually, I learned to ignore looks. Or his personality. Or his constant belittling.

I reminded myself every day that my life could be a hundred times worse. My first few months in space, at that awful brothel at the ass-end of the galaxy, were far worse. Being with Gant was tolerable. I mostly ignored him while I learned how to be a space pirate. I learned how to navigate and pilot right away. Because he was the cheapest son of a bitch in the sector, I also discovered how to fix almost every system on the ship.

Occasionally, my fury at him would flare. How dare he think he owned me? How could he justify using me for his lust? How could he assume I actually liked him? All he had to do was give one ounce of thought to our origin story. He had to know I harbored hatred, right?

My days with him were endless until we were hired to make a pickup from another pirate ship—Captain Thantose's ship, the *Ataraxia*. When I met his female, Brin, and the other Earth females on the ship, I assumed their relationships with their males were the same as Gant and me. Until I saw them together. Thantose loved Brin and treated her like she was the most precious thing this side of Antares.

When he realized what was going on with Gant and me, he offered an outrageous sum to buy me, then brought me aboard his ship. Thantose, his crew, and their human women nursed me back to emotional health. It helped that Brin's story had similarities to my own. She'd been abducted so very young. My heart bled for her.

After a few months, I'd recovered enough of my sanity and self-esteem to go off on my own.

Thantose fronted me the money for the *Serenity*, and the rest is history. It's a two-person craft, but I never hired anyone to help me. I can do it all myself. I'm not long on trust.

Before I left, I gave myself a new name. Jessica Wright didn't seem fitting anymore. I was no more the eighteen-year-old who was abducted from South Dakota than I was Santa Claus.

At first, I considered naming my vessel the Phoenix, but I liked the mythology so much I appropriated the name for myself. I vowed I'd leave on my new ship and create a new life, that I'd rise from the ashes like the mythological bird.

I realize that even in my mental ramblings about my history, I glossed over the Synth part. As shitty as it was, it's probably the only reason Gant sold me. I was indispensable. He never would have let me go if it hadn't been for his addiction.

He'd developed quite a nasty habit. I guess it started like most drug habits start—with a taste here and there. But the tastes became bigger and more frequent and the effects quickly turned ugly. He lazed around in a dream state most of the day.

I wasn't scared about captaining the *Serenity* on my own because I'd been captaining Gant's ship alone for months. He was gone. Useless. There was one saving grace. When the habit really took hold, his demands for sex stopped.

When he'd get low on Synth, first he'd get irritable, then mean as a snake. I'd find us a job and make the run while he bellowed from his bed, ordering me around as if he knew what was going on. Toward the end, I even made his Synth buys for him, just to shut him up.

So, I'm no fan of the drug.

I remind myself that So'Lan isn't Gant and that he never bought street drugs. So far, he's been a good male. I'll see how long it lasts.

# Chapter Five

**S** o'Lan

I wake, but keep myself still. It's an old method I developed from childhood. Being on stealth-mode allows you to learn information others are keeping secret. They let things slip when they think you're sleeping.

My brain comes fully back online as I remember where I am—and why. I need to think. To figure out who these people are and what they want from me.

First, though, I pay attention to my surroundings. Again, Phoenix is draped across me, her leg bent, her thigh on mine. Her arm is thrown across my chest as if we've slept like this for *annums*.

I've never slept with a female before. Not until last night. I've only received a female as a reward. Our joinings were quick and focused on a quick resolution before my Master sent her to the next male for his reward.

Having Phoenix here by her own choice, wrapped in my arms, feels good. It's as if she belongs at my side, in my embrace.

I stroke her hair, like I did last night on the tree branch. It's silky, softer than mine. I allow myself one more moment to pretend this is real, that I have an authentic connection with one other living being. Then I tug her tighter and review every moment of what happened since the tribesman came upon us in the forest.

I know the moment Phoenix awakens. Her body stiffens and her head tips to inspect me.

"You're awake?" she asks. "How are you feeling?"

Before I can stop her, she rises from the bed platform, retrieves the water and some food, and sets it between us on the mattress.

I down three full cups of water. "Detoxing isn't easy. Sleeping helped," I tell her as I pat the exact spot she just vacated, indicating I want her to lie back down next to me.

"Eat," she says as her lips press together.

"Why?"

"Why? You haven't eaten more than two nutrition bars since you woke up from being sedated yesterday. You need your strength." She tips her chin toward the platter again. "Eat."

"Lie down, then I'll eat."

"Bully," she says with a smile. "No deal. You eat, *then* I'll lie down."

I've never seen her smile before. It seems an odd time for it to make an appearance. No matter the circumstances, I like it.

I also like that she's concerned about my health. I never received anyone's concern until I was jailed in that dungeon on Fairea. I knew the other gladiators in the cells next to me genuinely cared about me.

After our release, I allowed myself to feel the affection of everyone in the compound. I even learned how to return it. But somehow, there's something about Phoenix's actions that feels different. Deeper.

"It took me a while to get to sleep. My mind hasn't stopped spinning. I have some hypotheses," she says as she hands me a bowl of stew and several pieces of bread.

The food tastes terrific, perhaps because I'm starving. I use the flat bread to shovel in the tasty stew. It's cold but still delicious. When my stomach doesn't rebel, I keep eating. She was right. I needed this.

"Tell me your thoughts," I say around a mouthful of food.

"While you were somehow learning our hosts' language," she pauses, pops a small globelike fruit in her mouth, and chews, "I was taking inventory of the village. There are maybe thirty huts. Let's say there are four people per family, that's 120 souls, give or take."

She lies back on the bed and puts her hands under her head. After scraping the bottom of the wooden bowl with the bread and popping the last bite of food into my mouth, I lean over to set the empty platter on the floor.

I snake my arm under her head so she can use my bicep as a pillow, then tug her even closer.

"Go on," I urge.

"You're a gladiator. One of you against 120 of them isn't going to work. I'm nothing at hand-to-hand combat, so I'll be of no help whatsoever. If we could get our weapons back, that would be a different story. If some of them go out on a hunt again, how many of the remainder do you think you could take?"

"Twenty unarmed would be easy. Ten or twelve if they have spears, but all one of them needs is to get a good shot at me and it's all over."

She pouts and bites her fingernail as she thinks.

The body is an amazing creation. It has two purposes—maintaining life and procreation. I never dreamed of having a mate or family. Those thoughts were so far from the reality of a gladiator slave that dreaming of them would just make my life more miserable. A female was a reward. For sexual release and nothing more.

When I was in the dungeon only being fed meager rations every few days, my body funneled my limited supply of energy to my heart to keep it beating.

My hair became limp and dry, then fell out. My muscles lost most of their mass. My organs were on the verge of failure. And early in the process, my body quit supplying extra blood to my cock. Since my release, I guess the Synth kept my erections at bay. I haven't had an erection for *lunars*. Not since my incarceration in that black hell hole.

That's history, I guess, because my cock has risen to this occasion and is pressing against my loincloth in Phoenix's direction.

There are chinks in the wood where sunlight pours in. One ray of it slices across her face from her hairline to the corner of her mouth. She's beautiful.

She has no reason to like me. I've been curt and irritable. Yet, she acts as if she's over that.

I've never been one to ponder and think things through. Perhaps that's why I was so successful in the arena. I'm a male who relies on instinct and superior reflexes.

"I wonder where they've stashed our weapons," she says, frowning. "If we could find them—"

I don't mean to be disrespectful, but I lean up to get a better look at her pretty face, then cup her soft cheek in my palm. This startles her. Her gaze flicks to mine, her eyes wide, but she doesn't pull away. She doesn't order me to stop. She holds my gaze as her pink lips part.

With one extended claw, I trace one sharp line along the same path my palm just traveled. It's not enough to draw blood, just something to stop her mind in its tracks, to force her into this moment—with me. She sucks in a quick breath.

"So'Lan?"

She wants something from me. What? Reassurance? Validation that I know I'm crossing a line?

"I want to kiss you, Phoenix." I'm on my side, one hand supporting my head, the other on her cheek. I extend all my claws and drag them through her short, silken hair, then retract them and pet her. A purr erupts from deep in my chest. Yes, I want to kiss her, but I could spend all day just stroking her like this.

"Weird timing," she observes. She's not pulling away, though. She keeps her gaze on mine.

"Terrible timing," I agree, as I dip my head toward hers. Before our lips touch, I give her ample time to object. I cup both her cheeks in my palms, then continue on my journey as I watch her reactions.

Two shallow lines form between her brows as if she's deep in thought, puzzled, as she continues to watch my descent.

My purr is louder now, rumbling enough to cause the bed to quiver. When I'm too close to maintain eye contact, I shutter my eyes and then close the final distance to her mouth.

I hover barely a hair's breadth from touching her as I savor the feel of her warm breath on my lips. I memorize her scent, which still smells of the little round fruit she snacked on.

Finally, I brush her lips with mine. It's barely a graze, just to get the lay of the land as if I'm an explorer in uncharted territory. I am.

I pull away just far enough to announce, "Soft," as if I just made a groundbreaking scientific discovery.

That single word is the key to setting her free from being a spectator to a participant. Her arms surround me, her fingers curl around my shoulders.

"Soft," she echoes as her fingers burrow through my fur. Her gentle, seeking touch makes me shiver.

I ply her with close-lipped kisses. I've never kissed anyone before. Maybe my parents when I was a youngling, but I remember nothing about those *annums*. I never kissed the females who were sent to my cell after a win.

"I don't want to hurt you with my fangs," I admit.

She presses her mouth to mine and makes a soft smacking noise, then pulls away enough to tell me, "Let's learn how to navigate that."

Despite her tiny kiss and her hands clutching me tight, until this moment I wasn't certain she fully wanted this kiss. Now that she's given her blessing, I banish my hesitance.

My lips harden against hers, letting her know if she doesn't open to me, I will force myself inside. She sighs and parts her lips as she rolls onto her back. Her posture is a primitive invitation that makes my cock bob with interest.

I grunt when my tongue breaches her barriers and invades her mouth. Her taste is clean and slightly sweet.

"Ah!" she says in surprise.

Did I hurt her? I pull back, grab her shoulders to inspect her face. What just happened?

"Your tongue. The… texture."

This is bad. She's used to humans. She must be disgusted by my alien differences.

"It surprised me. Do it again."

Relief washes over me.

She moves toward me, pushing me onto my back and straddling me with her knees clasped to my sides.

"Kiss me." Her breath is warm against my lips as she waits for me to breach her again.

This time, even though she's ready for the scratch of my tongue, she sucks in a breath. But she doesn't pull away, doesn't tell me to stop. With her in this position, she is in control, so I keep exploring her.

It's almost a game, knowing when to advance, when to retreat. When to coax her with my tongue, when to pull back and brush her lips with mine. She's burrowed her fingers into my mane, her hands clutching me as if she doesn't want to let me go.

Phoenix wriggles on me, moving until her heated center lands directly on my cock.

Now it's my turn to be surprised. My eyes flash open at her bold move. Though we're both clothed, this female is riding me. The scent of her arousal is rich in the room. I can't pay attention to the kissing anymore. I want to tear her clothes off and taste her down below. That too is a new desire for me.

Controlling my urge to rip her clothes off, I explore lower, dragging my tongue from her mouth down the cords of her neck. I had no idea this was a sensitive zone, I was simply moving from one point on her body to another. But she sucks in a quick breath, telling me this excites her. As if her little noise was too subtle, she grinds against my cock to make certain I know how much she likes it.

Perhaps it's the location. Maybe it's the rough burr of my tongue, but when I attend to this spot it arouses her, and her arousal calls to mine. Every muscle in my body is strung taut as a bow.

When I tongue her ear, her body freezes, then shivers. For the swiftest moment, I wonder if I've trespassed into a no-go zone, but her soft hiss of appreciation urges me to proceed. There are so many subtleties and nuances I never experienced with my female rewards. What I did with them was quick and functional. Phoenix is teaching me the feminine body is a target-rich environment. I vow to learn every spot on her flesh that makes her moan and writhe.

The sounds of the village drift to my ears. My tail flicks in irritation as two tribesmen engage in a loud debate as they walk by our hut. We're expected for a feast tonight. Our time is not our own. Besides, we have things to talk about.

I kiss her hard. Once, twice, three times.

"I want to finish this when the timing is right, pretty Phoenix," I tell her as I roll her off me. I don't like the separation, so I press a kiss to the top of her nose, then hurry back to kiss each eyelid.

"Right. Right," she says, shaking her head as if she's trying to return to sanity. "We need to plan our escape. What just happened here is madness. It shouldn't happen again."

Shouldn't happen again? Why? But I don't ask. Perhaps she's right.

No matter, we need to discuss our options. Where were we when we interrupted ourselves with that kiss? Ah yes, weapons.

"There's an even bigger problem than finding weapons," I say, my voice soft. I hate to bring this up because the bigger problem is her.

"What?"

"When we arrived, all the females were clothed. The two who were sent with food and water had removed their tops. Clearly, the tribe thinks I'm someone I'm not. Whoever they think I am, they want me to choose one of their females as a mate.

"I thought I was keeping you alive by insisting you are mine, but perhaps that was a tactical error. You are now the only thing standing in the way of me mating one of the tribe's females."

I've turned my head and have been watching her absorb my words. I see the exact moment my meaning becomes clear.

"I'm good for nothing. No. Less than that. I'm in the way," she says, then chews her bottom lip.

"Exactly. From this moment forward, we have to stay together no matter what. If we're separated, you won't be safe."

"I agree. Without my blaster, I'm defenseless."

"We don't know their endgame," I say. "We need to play along. Figure out what they want and find a way to stay alive until we can escape."

With perfect timing, there's a soft knock on the door. I swiftly rise to a sitting position on the edge of the bed and push Phoenix behind me as I say "Enter". This time, two different females enter. Like the last pair, their breasts are on full display as they each carry in two heavy buckets of steaming water.

Giggling, they motion for me to join them near the doorway.

"We'll wash you, Great Kirokai," the one with the longest black hair says as, in invitation, she lifts a sponge toward me.

When I don't move, the other pleads, "Please, Great Kirokai, let us do our duty or our families will be shamed." She slides to the floor in the same posture the others used earlier—on her belly.

I don't want the females to be punished, but I don't want to humiliate Phoenix.

What just happened in our bed was just a kiss, but for me, it changed everything. I'm not certain of everything the tribe wants or expects from me, but they want me to mate one of their young females. I won't play along with that deception for a moment longer.

"You are lovely. Both of you." I imagine Phoenix's expression as she sits behind me. I doubt it's a happy one. "I will not be taking a mate," I say firmly. "Please leave."

Both of them rise to a kneeling position, then gracefully stand as if they've practiced all their lives for this moment. Their eyes are luminous with unshed tears. I've shamed them, perhaps worse. When I see the chief tonight, I'll have to find a way to explain things, so these females aren't punished.

When the door closes behind them I say, "We're going to have to discuss how to deal with this." I rise, then turn to Phoenix and extend my arm.

"They may be treating you like a god, but by the look on the priest's face, your position is precarious. Maybe we should wait at least until after tonight? Get the lay of the land?"

"Yes." I nod my head in agreement. "Do you want me to bathe you, or give you privacy?"

She cocks her head, giving my question more thought than it deserves.

"No one has ever bathed me before. Besides, I'm not exactly sure what to do with a bucket. Bathe me." She looks amused, as if ordering me to bathe her is her heart's desire.

Not ten *minimas* ago, I terminated our kiss. Now I'm going to bathe her? Perhaps the Synth has done permanent damage to my brain. But I'm not going to change my mind. I'm going to seize the opportunity.

Extending my arm again, I motion for her to join me near the buckets. When she moves to pull her top off, I shake my head, my gaze never leaving hers.

"Let me." My purr starts again, vibrating in my chest without warning while my cock points toward her like an arrow aiming at its target.

"So'Brash," she says, her lips tipped into a lazy smile.

"You were in the *Serenity* for days. You've been tramping through the forest. I'm simply offering help." I smile wide enough to expose the tips of my fangs.

"I see. You're ever the gentlemale," she says with a grin as she steps toward me.

I spin her to face toward the back of the hut, then pull her against my chest. I like this position. Although it deprives me of her pretty face, it gives me complete access to every part of her.

She'd already removed her leather vest. As I tug her shirt over her head, I pause for a moment, considering keeping her arms trapped in the fabric. I want to assert complete control over her, although I don't need to. She hasn't resisted me in any way.

After tossing the garment onto the bed, for a moment I imagine using my sharp claws to rend her black leather pants, slicing them from waist to ankle, rather than tugging them down. There's something about Phoenix, maybe it's her tiny form, that triggers something primal in me, but I push my barbaric urges away. I slip my thumbs under the waistband of her pants, hit the black leather pants' autozip, and pull them down and off.

Clasping her shoulders, I step back to get a good look at her. She's in her bra and panties. I've seen porn on the Intergalactic Database when I was researching other things. I might have looked longer than was necessary before I flipped to where I intended to go.

There are millions of pictures of nude and scantily clad females, some in exotic lingerie. None stirred me like Phoenix in her skimpy white underwear.

Half of me wants to rip it off. The other half likes the somewhat chaste, very sexy sight of her like this. I picture slipping aside the scant piece of fabric between her legs and plunging into her slick depths while she's still partially clothed.

I remove the rest of her clothes, though, and simply look at her.

"Beautiful," I say, my voice breathless and husky. Sometimes in the barracks, when the gladiators shared a batch of homemade brew, my fangs would get in the way of my words. I sounded muffled. I'm talking that way now. I'm drunk on the sight of her.

When she turns to look at me over her shoulder, I tuck her close and claim her mouth, spearing my tongue into her. She opens to me, denying me nothing.

For a moment, I'd thought what happened between us on the bed just now was a fluke. That's clearly not true. Even though she insisted it shouldn't happen again, she wants my touch, desires my kisses.

I pull away. "Let me bathe you."

I bend to soak the crimson sponge in the water, then stand and squeeze it over her shoulder, watching the liquid as it spills over her pale skin.

Over and over, I repeat these actions, allowing the dirt and dust of the past few days to slide into the hardened soil beneath her feet and flow out under the edge of the hut.

I've never been allowed this much time, this much intimacy with a female. It's glorious to be with her like this. To allow the silence to become comfortable. To be granted free rein over her flesh.

I turn her and am honored when her gaze doesn't flinch from mine. The other Earthers in the compound don't like to expose themselves. Nudity is frowned upon in their culture.

Phoenix isn't shy. She has a small smile playing at the corners of her mouth as she watches me.

"Like what you see, So'Sexy?" she asks. How can her voice be both proper and forward at the same time?

I hold her pretty gray gaze in mine so she doesn't miss the sincerity of my answer. "The most beautiful thing I've ever seen."

## Phoenix

I've been through a lot of crazy moments since I was abducted ten years ago. The abduction itself was both crazy and terrifying. Pretending my time as a sex slave was just a horrible, bizarre dream helped me get through some awful days.

But right now? Being held hostage by a tribe of green aliens who think my friend is a god? This takes the cake. No. Not really. What takes the cake is that he's bathing me with the sweetest strokes imaginable.

Actually, what's most astonishing is the way he's looking at me, like I'm the most important thing in the universe. The most surreal part of it is that I like him and am drawn to him and I'm feeling sensual yearnings deep in my pelvis for the first time in a decade.

The awareness makes me tremble.

I feel raw, exposed. So much so that I step closer and manhandle him so he faces away from me.

"Remove your loincloth," I order. My voice sounds casual. To my ears, it sounds as if I do this for a living.

*No wonder they bow before him and think he's a god. Just look at him.* I try to push the thought away, but it's already spiked through my thoughts and I can't unthink it.

He may have been emaciated and near death a few months ago, but there's nothing lean about him now. He's pumped and muscular from his broad shoulders to his narrow waist to his beefy ass. His tail twitches, just once. I don't know what it means, but I vow to figure out all his little tells.

My palms itch to trace the indents at the side of his hips, or perhaps the crease down the line of his spine, or the rock-hard curves of his shoulders.

A shaft of sunlight slashes across his golden, furred back from his right shoulder to his left hip. I want to trace the path with my tongue. Never in my wildest dreams did I imagine wanting to lick fur. But So'Lan's magnificent body is irresistible.

I could stand here and debate with myself, or wonder why, after ten years in space, I've suddenly found a male I would actually choose to share my body with. But that sounds like a fool's errand. I'll never figure it out.

Well, it really isn't that hard to figure out. He's the first male, human or alien, who has considered my needs and sought not only my consent, but also my opinion.

I soak the sponge in water and squeeze it onto his shoulder, watching the rivulets slide down his back, making patterns in his fur. The wet fur turning a bit darker than its dry counterpart.

Once his back is wet, I get the brilliant idea to order, "Put your hands on your head."

This huge male, at least a foot taller than me and so strong he could break me in half, follows my instruction before it's barely out of my mouth.

Look. At. Him.

That's one gorgeous male.

I lean closer and sniff. He smells delicious, like the warm, rich scent of a grassy field on a sunny day. Using one finger, I trace the bolt of light from his shoulder in a slash across his back. Yes, it's velvety, just as I discovered last night on that narrow limb.

Wanting to know his body more intimately, I step closer. So close the tips of my nipples drag across the satiny bristle of his fur. Now, I give in to temptation and follow that streak of sunlight with my tongue. He's too tall for my tongue to reach his shoulder. But I stand as high as I can, then trace a warm path through his fur.

The tip of my tongue burrows through his soft fur to the skin below. His taste is divine. It's a different flavor than his mouth entirely. It's more earthy, more real, more masculine, if that's possible.

He's standing perfectly still. I get it. He probably doesn't want to jinx this, even though he's the one who put a screeching halt to the incendiary kiss we just shared on the bed.

Yes, okay, I was the one who said it shouldn't happen again. The timing really isn't good, but right now I don't care.

I've gotten to the end of my little sunbeam, but I'm not ready to stop. I want to keep going. There's a part deep inside that wants to *consume* him. He's not complaining.

I hunch lower, blazing a trail down, past his waist, all the way to his rounded ass. I nip it. No, this is no nip, this is a bite. Using the tip of one finger, I nudge his back and wait for him to bend forward.

The moment he complies, I bite him again. How did I tap this primitive part inside myself? I have no idea, but I don't force it away. No. I double down by gripping him by his hipbones and tenderly gnawing at him.

"So'Good," I breathe.

My words break the spell. He's no longer a furred, meaty statue. He turns in my arms, surrounds me in his embrace, and lifts me so we're face to face. In order to maintain our connection, I circle his waist with my legs.

My lids shock wide in surprise. I wonder if this was a mistake or perhaps the smartest thing I've ever done.

"I want you, So'Lan," I tell him, then press my lips to his and devour him in a kiss.

He hitches me against him and takes control.

His huge hands splay open against my back. One on my waist, one between my shoulder blades. His cock, no longer covered by a loincloth, is smashed between us.

"I want you. I want your cock inside me. I've never wanted anything as much as I want this," I say. The force of it shocks me. The *truth* of it shocks me. Surely no one who has been a slave could say such a thing, could they?

What slave hasn't prayed for freedom more than the very air they breathe? But I want this male, this kind, strong male, more than anything I've ever wanted in my life.

My nipples *ache* for him. My pussy *weeps* for him. I want him in my mouth and in my pussy and if I could, I'd figure out how to do both at the same time.

"They'll be coming for us soon," he says, then bends to nip those ferocious fangs along the cords of my neck.

"Then get to it, So'Slow."

He strides to the bed and lays me down. Instead of pouncing, he takes a step back.

"I'm aching over here," I scold, then whisper, "So'Mean."

"I'm memorizing over here, female."

I know he's playing with me, but his voice is rough. I decide it's from need.

"Open your legs."

The harsh command and the bright shine in his blue eyes make my channel clench. I follow his order without hesitation.

"Wider."

His purr stutters for a moment, then resumes—louder.

I open myself an inch. As desperate as I am, there's something about this teasing game that is so sexy I can't resist. I'm watching him lose his self-control with every inch I grant him.

"More." His voice is sand and gravel.

Another inch.

"Do I have to yank them open?" he puts just enough edge in his voice that my channel flutters with need.

In answer, I don't move.

He'd taken a step back to watch the Phoenix show. Now he pounces forward, grips my knees, and deliberately forces them wide.

Did I say force? Yes. The sexiest thing anyone has ever done. After my time in the sex shops on planet Numa, I never thought I'd enjoy sex again. I certainly never thought I'd be able to play, much less enjoy power exchange. It's different with So'Lan.

He's towering over me, his grip on my knees a smidge shy of pain. He leans over, putting that beautiful face only inches from mine, granting me a whiff of his intoxicating, masculine scent, then shocks me when he whispers in my ear, "Is this okay, Phoenix?"

He has no idea of my history. We've never shared tragic backstories, although I know some of his. But anyone who's kicked around the galaxy for more than a day knows all former slaves have... issues, and all Earth girls have been slaves. I never thought of the big, furred lion-man as sensitive, but he becomes more surprising with every passing minute.

"Breathe in through your nose, lion-man. You tell me."

All aliens can smell a female's arousal. Must be an evolutionary advantage.

He doesn't just take a sniff. He prowls lower on my body, places his shaggy head between my legs, and drinks in a huge gust of me. His mouth opens slightly to get a taste of my tang on the air. When it hits his tastebuds, his purr accelerates faster and louder.

I'd thought he tossed me on the bed so he could fuck me, but I was wrong. It looks like I'm what's for dinner. His maned head dips between my legs and he exhales hot blasts of air between my legs. When a stream of it hits my clit, I shiver and a soft, "Oh!" escapes me.

"That's right, little Phoenix," he rumbles. "I want your words. Tell me, now, if you want this."

Perhaps he's a master of torture, because he drags the silken tuft of hair from the point of his chin across my clit and down my slit, breathing out a forceful stream of warm air as he goes. First the satin slide of the hair, then the blast of hot air.

My body quivers in response as I grip his furred shoulders. "So'Lan, so good. Don't stop."

He does it again and again until I feel inches away from release, and he hasn't even touched me yet.

Without warning, he stabs his tongue into my channel. His tongue is thick and long, and the tiny feline spurs send a tingle through me. He laps for a moment until a deep, back-of-the-throat growl erupts from his mouth. It rumbles and vibrates through me until I quiver, my thighs clutching the sides of his head.

Was that a mini-orgasm? He hasn't even touched my clit.

He makes another non-threatening purr-growl in response, then rears back, stabs me with a questioning stare, then dips his head to attack my clit.

He may be attacking me down below, but he took that little intermission to check on me, make sure I was enjoying his attentions.

"Yes," I urge. It's all I have the energy to say.

He flicks the tip of my clit with swift strokes. I imagine this would feel amazing with a regular tongue. Because of his rasps, what he's doing is divine.

I'm greedy. I place my soles on the bed to gain better leverage so I can press myself up against him. He gets the hint, increases his pressure, then finds the magic spot on the side of the little bundle of nerves.

"So!" I can't scrape together the energy to speak the two syllables of his name.

He increases the pressure, then releases a long, low purr. It's that final vibration that forces me over the edge. I tumble on a slow roll toward ecstasy. My climax starts almost lazily, with a few meager spasms. He chases it, flicking and licking until the orgasm hits a second phase—a whole other level.

It's a powerhouse, darting through me like lightning. My fingers clench his soft mane as every muscle in my body vibrates in bliss.

Just when the rollercoaster ride is about to come to a stop, he nuzzles my greedy pleasure button with the velvety flat of his nose. I'm off for another round of soul-shattering pleasure so intense I call his name.

As I float back to reality, he slides up to lie at my side. I memorize everything about this moment, perhaps because in the back of my mind I wonder if the tribe is out there heating water in a pot big enough to boil an Earth female.

His mane is soft and thick. From far away, it's a mass of chestnut fur. Up close, though, I can see the variations in each hair. They're all slightly different colors. Toward his back, they're tipped with darker bronze. It's beautiful.

One of his rounded ears flicks. Is it a question?

"So good. Give me a moment."

I don't want to talk right now. I just want to bask in the sexy aftershocks flickering through my body. And take his inventory.

There's a little black dot where each whisker emerges from around his nose. Now that I pay attention, I think I felt them tickling my thighs earlier. I was too focused on other things to notice.

He catches my gaze as if he has something important to say, then lazily, almost as if he's in slow motion, he opens his mouth, exposing those dangerous fangs. He unfurls that feline tongue of his and licks his chops.

Be still my heart.

That is the sexiest thing I've ever seen. He's savoring me. My taste.

"Delicious," he husks, as if the meaning of his actions was too subtle for me.

"Come fuck me, you sexy beast," I say as I roll onto my back in invitation.

His brows furrow in a look of hurt.

"And I mean that in the best way possible," I amend.

He chuffs, then swiftly moves between my legs.

With perfect timing, there's a soft knock on the door.

# Chapter Six

**P**hoenix

He leaps up, flips the colorful blanket over me, then stalks to the door. He can't unlock it—that's done from the outside. He yanks the door open as soon as he hears the rasp of the wooden latch being raised.

There's only one maiden this time. She's naked from the waist up, but wears a headdress similar to the chief's. I wonder if she's a relative.

She walks in, but there's something about her posture that's different from the other females who've entered our little hut. She's not as submissive. She's standing taller than them.

She misses nothing. First, she takes a dramatic sniff in through her humanoid nose, then drills me with a knowing stare. Point taken. She doesn't miss the scent of Phoenix in the air. Then she spends an inordinate amount of time looking So'Lan up and down and up again.

I can only see his magnificent golden backside, his tail flicking in irritation. She's being treated to the full monty. He was just about to mount me. Even with the intrusion, I imagine he's still hard as stone. By his tall, proud stance, he's not embarrassed. If I had to put a word on it, I'd say he's defiant.

"Kirokai," she says with a slight bow of her head. I notice she doesn't preface the name with the word "great." "My father sent me to invite you to a feast in your honor. You can bring your slave. I've brought clean clothing."

Her back is ramrod straight as she dips her head slightly in deference, then hands him a neatly folded pile of colorful clothing.

After she backs out of the door and closes it, So'Lan moves to the bed, sorts through the clothing, and hands me my garments.

His stare doesn't leave my body when I flip off the blanket and rise out of bed. His cock is still hard and beaded with pre-cum. His aquamarine gaze burns for me.

"Come here, So'Hard. I'll take care of you. Take the edge off."

He gives a quiet, rueful grunt from the back of his throat.

"When you and I come together for the first time, it won't be quick and hurried. I will slake my hunger at my leisure."

"I could use my mouth? My hand? I don't want to leave you hanging," I say, although the last way I'd describe that magnificent, golden cock is hanging. It's hard as steel, pointing at the ceiling, and bobbing in excitement.

"I'll wait." He leans forward and catches my bottom lip between his fangs. It's so exciting, hanging on the cusp of danger and pleasure, that I suck in a gasp of surprise. "Later," he promises.

"They must really think you're some kind of god," I breathe several minutes later when I look over to find him fully dressed.

His headdress is a foot higher than the chief's. I may not know much about primitive jungle tribes, but I imagine headgear is kind of like cock size. The bigger one always wins.

Unlike the chief's, which looked to be made of colorful textiles and feathers, So'Lan's is golden. And by golden, I don't mean paint. I might not be an expert in metallurgy, but I think this is the real deal.

It's over a foot tall, with golden wings that remind me of the way they portrayed the Roman god Mercury. The skullcap that hugs his head doesn't have cutouts where a humanoid's ears would be. This was made to leave room for a lion's rounded ears because they sit higher on his head.

It's amazing and makes him look regal. Just wearing it has made him stand a bit taller, prouder.

"So'Gorgeous," I breathe. "If every female in the village hadn't set her sights on you before, they certainly will now."

My gaze sweeps down his body. He's wearing nothing but a crimson leather kilt that doesn't reach his knees. He's a sight to behold.

On the other hand, I think the tribe dug deep into their Goodwill box for my outfit. It's an oversized threadbare castoff dress. Perhaps it was nice in its day. It's made of the colorful textiles the tribe seems so fond of.

"So gorgeous," he repeats my words. If he wasn't looking straight at me like he wants to eat me up, I'd think he was teasing. But I guess that old saying about beauty being in the eye of the beholder is right. His warm expression says he'd love to tear this rag off my body and resume what we started on the bed.

Soon, two males with spears escort us the few feet toward the firepit. Yes, there's a large pot over the fire. No, it's not filled with boiling water waiting for me. It smells like food.

It seems everyone in the tribe is assembled. When So'Lan arrives, a murmur moves through the crowd and they all bow their heads.

"Welcome Great Kirokai," the chief says. Not to be outdone, he's no longer wearing the headdress he had on when we arrived. I guess that was his everyday wear. For this gala event, he's also wearing gold. It's dripping with gems on the skullcap and boasts golden horns reminiscent of a water buffalo. It's not as tall as the Great Kirokai's, though. Rank has its privilege.

The high priest steps forward and intones, "Welcome. We have waited many generations for your return, Great Kirokai. We have never lost sight of your instructions and have remained ever-prepared."

He indicates a chair for So'Lan to sit on. The males who walked us here, point me to a spot on the other side of the fire.

As soon as he realizes what's happening, So'Lan raises his hand to interrupt the priest, who does not hide his irritation at this perceived slight. So'Lan beckons me to his side, continuing the "come here" motion until he's obeyed. Since he's the only person in the assemblage other than the chief and the priest afforded a chair, I don't take offense at having to sit at his feet.

"Our females, as instructed," the priest continues, still piercing So'Lan with an irritated gaze at his impertinence of changing the seating arrangements, "are kept pure until their eighteenth rotation, so upon your arrival, you would have your choice of the ripest and most beautiful our tribe has to offer.

"In your absence, our artisans created this headdress. We hope it is adequate for your needs. We duly noted you love the golden substance."

While he was speaking, he kept bobbing his head. It seemed the downstroke was to offer his obeisance. The upstroke was to hint at his resistance.

"Before the feast and the presentation of our females, our hunters will bestow your tribute."

He waves his hand, and from off to the side, a line of young males approaches. Each is carrying either a large trinket or a platter full of smaller ones.

There are golden statues depicting what must be every animal on the asteroid. Horned bovine, spotted felines, and of course, gators. Some of these figurines have to be over a foot tall. By the way the males' arms are straining, it appears they're not hollow.

The tote board in my head is trying to add up what this booty must be worth. I deal in stolen goods. Sometimes Thantose sends jobs my way transporting art and antiquities, like the job I went to Sanctuary for. What I've already seen has to be worth millions.

Then the younger males step forward with platters, also gold, laden with jewelry, cups, plates, and utensils.

The chief stops a few of the males and pulls things from their treasure trove. A bejeweled goblet, a plate, a knife, and fork. He sets them near So'Lan's feet.

When the parade is over, they pile the remaining booty near the fire in an awesome display of wealth.

"I hope this pleases you, my Lord," the chief says, his hands in the palms-together posture of prayer.

"Yes," So'Lan says.

**So'Lan**

The chief's daughter approaches, her eyes downcast, her hands filled with a golden pitcher. Kneeling, she fills the jeweled goblet to the brim with a red liquid, then offers it to me with both hands.

For half a moment, I wondered if it was blood. Perhaps the bizarre nature of today's events has confused me. One deep whiff and I'm certain this isn't blood, it's fermented spirits.

No matter how foul, or how rotten the produce we were fed as gladiators, we always found a way to ferment the food into spirits in one of the rear cells. I used to enjoy partaking.

A gladiator's life was filled with misery from lifting weights until our bodies ached, to fighting in the hot sun to the point of exhaustion, to being injured or having to kill. Homebrew and the reward of female flesh were the only bright spots in my decades as a gladiator.

At times I drank as much as I could pour down my throat. It hits me like a hammer to realize I showed glimpses of addiction back then. Of course, there was never enough brew to go around, much less enough to keep me as drunk as I might have wished.

It was only after my release from the dungeon, with the Synth plentiful and freely given, that I had the opportunity to see the depths to which I would sink to feed my need—which was endless.

I reached for the golden goblet without even thinking. It's in my hand, the heady scent of wine wafting to my nostrils.

I war with myself for a moment, even as every eye is upon me. I realize with a clarity I've never before experienced that I'm at a choicepoint. One of the biggest and most meaningful of my life.

I could sip this wine. Or, rather, I could swig it down in the manner I have a hundred times before. Then one thing could lead to another. I am, after all, worshipped here. If I asked for wine to be served with breakfast, lunch, and dinner, it would be gladly offered.

I picture myself as I must have looked in Pherutan the medic's office only a few days ago. I recall roaring at him so loudly he couldn't hide his shock. I lifted him and held him off his feet, threatening him with my words and deeds, all in search of a drug. A drug that was destroying my mind and my soul as surely as it was affecting my body.

With a flash of clarity I've never had before, I hand the golden goblet back to the pretty tribeswoman.

"Thank you. I prefer water," I tell her.

Relief flows through me like a fast-running stream. I don't want any substance to play with my mind. I want no drugs to fuel my thoughts or steal my soul. I wish to retain my lucidity.

Somehow I know I will never in the future use a substance under the false belief that it will make anything better. I'm done with it. It's as if I hear the clang of metal doors in my mind, putting an end to that sordid chapter of my life.

I glance at Phoenix, and by the close-lipped smile on her face, it's clear she observed my struggle and approves of my decision.

"Now for the presentation of the females. You may choose one immediately or watch and observe how they behave during the feast."

I open my mouth to tell them I'm not here to choose a female, but I remind myself Phoenix and I had decided not to address this until we'd had time to assess our position.

Ten females walk in a line toward me. They wear only the shortest skirts and, other than golden jewelry, are otherwise nude. Each is given time to turn in front of me, trying to show herself off to best advantage. At the end of her display, she removes her jewelry and places the pieces in the pile as tribute.

The meek ones bend their knees to place their items on the pile. The bolder females bend over, their backsides facing me, giving me a view of *all* their wares. I glance at Phoenix, who is glowering at them through narrowed eyes.

The display saddens me. Who came before me? Was it one or many of my race? Now that I have time to look around this area, I see totems at intervals between the circle of huts. They all have depictions of males like me. Unmistakably Ton'arr.

They demanded tribute? Ordered that all females of the tribe be kept pure until their eighteenth birthday so they would be ripe and ready upon their return? It disgusts me.

"I hope our females please you, Kirokai. That your trip through the stars was worth the effort to bless our meager tribute. Let's feast," says the chief.

I'm far more absorbed in the people around me than the food they are plying me with. I watch the interactions of the tribe, assessing their weapons and their readiness to fight. In my head, I count their numbers, trying to figure out what their thoughts are about me and how angry they will be if I reject their daughters.

When I glance at Phoenix, I'm surprised to find her eyes bright with interest at her surroundings. I expected her to be pouting, relegated as she is to the position of slave. Having to sit in the dirt at my feet rather than on a small, armless chair similar to the one the chief has me sitting on.

She's a smart female. Strong. I admire her will. I want to get to know her better.

I feed her the choicest bites of food, which she takes with her mouth, never failing to lick my fingers or close her soft lips over them. I've been rock hard since the first lick of her pretty pink tongue.

"Have you had your fill of the finest food our tribe has to offer?" the chief asks from my left as the priest on the other side of Phoenix says, "I trust you enjoyed our efforts."

"Excellent," I nod, even as I hope the evening's festivities will end so I can complete what Phoenix and I started in our hut.

"I hope you will find this next part of the evening as much of a treat as I do," the chief says with a sparkle in his eyes. He claps his hands twice and after a flurry of activity, all the children in the village converge into the space between where I'm sitting and the fire.

The children, full of enthusiasm, act out everything I've wondered about my origin story.

The chief's wife, in a long colorful skirt, narrates how the Great Kirokai came to the asteroid on his fiery chariot. The children sing and dance, pantomiming the male's arrival. They show how he taught them to fashion spears out of metal.

I grunt in displeasure. Must the more civilized species always bring death and destruction with them wherever they visit?

The chief's wife, Celletta, explains how he told them he was a god. I grunt yet again, having trouble hiding my anger. I guess someone coming from the stars would seem like a god to these primitives.

Then the onlookers all sing a doleful song about how Kirokai threatened to leave, and how the head priest begged him to stay.

The next morning, Kirokai was gone, but the priest said he promised to return. The priest relayed all Kirokai's decrees so the village would be prepared for his return. His instructions were that if he didn't return, the priest would get the first choice of female. The priest in the story was a hero, and Kirokai remained a venerated god who vowed to come back to shepherd the tribe into greatness.

It's at this point that the chief turns to me and asks, "Are you pleased with this feast, Great Kirokai? Do you approve of your gifts?"

The crowd silences itself as they all lean forward to hear my pronouncement.

They are a handsome people, with high cheekbones and intelligent eyes. On information passed down from generation to generation, they have prepared for my arrival. They seem desperate to please me, which makes sense. They believe I'm a god.

If I were a god, how would I react? The answer seems obvious. If I were a deity, I would be benevolent.

I stand and slowly turn my head from one side of the crowd to the other. I take my time, looking each person in the eye as I nod.

"You have pleased me," I tell them in a low, solemn voice. "Who would not be satisfied to have their instructions followed so well? The golden gifts are beautiful. The food was well-prepared and delicious. The play was acted with deep feeling."

Emotion wells in my breast. I've been a gladiator my entire life. I received adulation in the arena for my prowess at hurting others. I enjoyed the praise. Who could hear their name shouted in appreciation and not allow it to fill their head with pride?

But this is different. Although I'm being venerated by accident, I have an opportunity here. I can have a positive impact on these primitive people. It takes me the tiniest portion of a moment to decide to use my power to improve these people's lives.

"Will all the actors come to stand before me?" I ask as I indicate the space between where I'm standing and the roaring fire.

At first, the children glance worriedly at their parents. When I motion to where I want them, they reluctantly come forward, obviously fearful of me. Phoenix and I discussed this. My status as a god might be the only thing keeping us alive. I dare not jeopardize that, but I can change the dynamic.

I see a little girl in her mother's lap, clinging to her shoulders. I recall this little one, because her hair is unusual, almost as light as Phoenix's. I know she participated in the play.

"You," I say in a calm voice. "I want you up here, too."

Her mother looks terrified, but rises with the little one in her arms. Both of them join the group of children in front of me.

"I was very entertained by your production," I say, my words pouring out quickly to dispel their fear. "I want to reward you for your fine work. I'd like the children of each family to gather together."

When they are assembled into family groups, I choose one small gold trinket from the overflowing pile of wealth, and gift it to the youngest child in each family, along with a soft pat on each of their heads.

I wonder what it would have been like when I was a child if someone I revered had taken a moment's notice of me, had praised me, had given me even the smallest gift.

All the children's faces are shining in happiness. It appears that gold is plentiful on this asteroid, that the worth of the items is no more than if they had been fashioned out of wood. But receiving a gift from me, the traveler from afar, might be something they remember fondly fifty *annums* from now.

My heart overflows with happiness, knowing I bestowed this upon them.

The crowd breaks out in spontaneous cheering. When I see the adults' faces, I notice they cheer for me, but that's not what I want. I've been the object of cheering before. It's always been laced with bloodlust. I don't need their adulation.

I smile at the group, not worrying about showing my fangs. The females I bedded as a gladiator would flinch when they saw my fangs. These tribespeople have grown up seeing a face like mine on every totem in and around the village.

With an open smile on my face, I extend my arms and clap toward the group of children. It's a silent message for the tribe to give praise to their own offspring.

During my speech, both the chief and priest stood alongside me.

"And now, Kirokai? Will you choose your mate among the most pure and beautiful our village has to offer?"

"It is with reluctance I must admit my sorrow that I have not visited sooner to tell you your beautiful daughters did not have to await my return. I have chosen another. My mate. Phoenix," I say with a smile as I motion her to join me.

## Phoenix

I enjoyed So'Lan's speech as I watched him glow with pride. It was clear he loved heaping praise at the children and filling them with positive self-esteem.

The lion-man I met in Dhoom's office only a few days ago was not only an angry, grumpy, angsty male on his knees because of his addiction. His eyes were dull, and not just because of his physical condition. He had lost a part of himself on the journey from gladiator to addict. It appears a big part of him died in that underground dungeon.

His comrades cared for him, but it was obvious their respect could only be described in the past tense. Watching him in his foot-high golden headdress is exciting because under its weight, the male he was meant to be has begun to bloom.

He is stepping into a position of power and admiration.

When my attention turns to the chief and priest, it's like I'm watching a horror movie as they seem to move in slow-motion. They pull small knives from their belts. I thought they were ornamental, but by the look in the two males' eyes, they don't have anything decorative in mind.

Within seconds, eight warriors leap from their places in the audience and converge to surround So'Lan and me.

"We worshipped you for generations," the priest seethes, "we hammered the golden metal into jewelry. We denied our females their choice of mates during their prime. All this because of your decree. Now with a wave of your hand, you tell us you've changed your mind? For that?" He slashes his hand toward me in a dismissive motion. "No!"

"We cannot allow this. This is a step too far," the chief agrees.

Two warriors have moved to my side and are holding short knives at my throat. Our position is precarious. I'm praying So'Lan takes an extra moment to gather his thoughts. If he turns around and sees me like this, I think he's going to lose his shit. Which means we both might lose our lives.

He swivels his head toward me. I watch as different emotions cross his face. First, his eyes widen in surprise, then they narrow in anger, then his muscles tense. It's as if I can read his mind. I know as sure as I'm breathing that he's preparing to leap to my rescue.

"Great Kirokai," I say loudly, then repeat, "my great Kirokai." I hope the panic in my gaze shouts how serious I am. "I know you to be a calm statesman." I emphasize those last two words, hoping he gathers my meaning.

"Certainly you can work with the venerated chief and the esteemed priest of this, your most treasured tribe."

I can see the moment he realizes the stakes. He's been alone his whole life. Every decision he's ever made reflected on him and him alone. Now, though, his choices have very real consequences for me. Considering the two knives at my throat, I'd say the ramifications could be life and death.

He bends his head, takes a breath, then looks at first one and then the other of the two males at his side.

"Let us discuss this like the leaders we are," he says. "Like males of honor."

The two native males nod in agreement.

"Come to my hut," the chief offers, then calls to the two warriors guarding me. "Put her in the punishment hut."

## So'Lan

Punishment hut? It takes all my conscious effort not to roar in anger, not to strike down the two males at my sides. I'm a gladiator, trained from a young age to kill. I've fought one against many more times than I can count. I have fangs and claws that these tribesmen don't possess. I might not be able to kill every male in the tribe, but I can kill their leaders before they draw their next breath.

But no. Phoenix is at their mercy. For the first time in my life, bravery does not equal fighting. Bravery does not equal risking my life. Bravery right this moment means taking a calm breath and appeasing these ignorant males. I'll calmly accompany them if it gives me time to discover how to free my female.

We enter the chief's hut, which is overly warm and smells of a cloyingly sweet herb. His mate is here. She's the elder who narrated the children's production.

"Excuse the smell," she says as she repeatedly billows the cloth door open and closed to air out the hut. "I'm a healer. This smell is an herb we use to deaden the pain of the sick."

I'm thankful she leaves the flap open. The last thing I need is for my thoughts to swirl like they do from Synth.

"Our young females keep themselves pure," the chief repeats. "They are trained from one generation to the next on how to move with grace and agility, how to serve a mate. We've followed your instructions precisely for all these years.

"To change your mind now is an insult to the beautiful females of our tribe."

If I were a different male, I would consider their offer. A different male would enjoy being treated like a god by a female who spent her childhood learning how to please him. A different male would consider it foolish to choose a little Earther who teases constantly and challenges frequently.

I'm not a different male. I don't want another female. I want to explore where things are going with the clever little Earther. *My* clever little Earther.

I'm stunned by the realization that I'm willing to risk my life to keep her alive. I may not have known her for long, but I have feelings for her. I need to think my way out of this—for both our sakes.

These tribesmen call me a god, but they argue my decree. My status here only goes so far. If I refuse them outright, Phoenix and I might both die.

"Even gods have weaknesses," I admit with a smile. "Despite all my power, I've fallen for the little female." I shrug. "Isn't that the way it is? I can fly through the sky, learn your language in a matter of moments, and slay my enemies with a bolt of lightning. Yet I have affection for the little female despite the obvious beauty of your tribeswomen." I stare first at the chief, then the priest. My words were true about slaying my enemies—if I could just get my hands on our weapons.

What do you know? I see our backpacks lying under the chief's raised platform bed. Later, I'll figure out how to sneak them out of here. Right now, I need all my faculties to talk my way out of my current predicament. By the looks on these males' faces, I'm not doing a very good job.

"Don't blame a male for thinking with his cock when a female is concerned, right?" I laugh, like I'm letting them in on a little joke.

They're glowering. The priest's hand edges toward the knife in his belt.

"Tell me, how do the males of your tribe resolve a dispute over a female?" I ask.

"Contests," the priest says. His eyes brighten. It's the exact moment he realizes he can make life hell for me without it looking personal.

Before the tension escalates, and after a perfunctory protest, I agree to a contest. We discuss the rules for another *hoara*. When I suggested it, I knew they wouldn't let a god get away with an easy challenge. As every *minima* ticks by, I watch the priest piling on the difficulties. That's okay. I'm a Ton'arr. A gladiator. And I have something to fight for. Phoenix.

"Until the contest, I have a request," the chief says after we hammer out the details. "Your cock may want the pale female, but you haven't even considered our females. We've waited a long time for your return," the chief says. "We've followed your edicts and decrees just as you laid them out many rotations ago. I beg of you, Kirokai, give us a chance. If not all the females of the tribe, then just one. Zendaya, my daughter. She's the beauty who served you the maraberry wine."

His stare is so hard on me, it's as if he could drill right through me. I don't believe he'll bend on this.

"What do you ask of me?"

"She will pack a lunch for the both of you and take you to the tribe's favorite watering hole. You will be assured privacy. You will talk to her, get to know her, give her a chance to steal your heart."

Since it's very clear no is not an option, I nod in agreement.

"And to ease your mind that the pale female will be safe, I will have her protected by my best warrior, Ebudan. I will have him show her the hunting grounds where the *eltoks* graze. I will ensure her safe return on the life of my daughter, Zendaya."

The chief is nothing if not persistent. He not only wants me to bond with his daughter, he's ensuring we'll have enough privacy for me to take her virginity. I imagine if I were foolish enough to do that, I'd be forced to mate her the moment we returned to the village.

By the same token, he's hoping Phoenix will bond with the warrior. He's crafty and smart. I can't wait to get both this courtship ritual and the challenge contest out of the way. I may be a gladiator, but the contest they have planned for me is not going to be easy.

"Yes," I say. "But tonight I share lodgings with the pale female."

The chief pauses. It's almost as if I could read his mind as he figures out how to deny my request, but after a moment, he nods his agreement.

# Chapter Seven

**P**hoenix

Shit! So much for being a god. Where does that get you if you can't pick who you want to mate? I've been around the block enough times to know there's always a catch.

I startle myself with the realization that I was just lamenting the fact that So'Lan isn't allowed to mate me. Am I crazy? Have I lost my mind?

I've been in outer space for ten years. Ten mostly miserable years with a few brief glimpses of calm. Not happiness, mind you. Not joy, but calm. It's the best I could hope for under the shitty circumstances of my life.

I've known So'Handsome for two days, well two days where he wasn't comatose, and I'm considering mating him. I am officially, certifiably insane.

Being turned on is one thing. That was a pleasant, well more than pleasant, surprise. But having any type of relationship with him is something entirely different. I need to keep a lid on my emotions.

I take inventory of the punishment hut, which is small and sturdy. It's no bigger than a closet, and there are two armed males standing outside the locked door. They've manacled my wrists and ankles. The fact that my shackles are made of gold means nothing. Golden handcuffs are still handcuffs.

So'Lan looked pissed when they decreed he needed to mate one of the tribe's females. I hope he holds his temper. The chief and priest didn't look like they'd let him get away with much. I have a feeling they can't wait for him to make one wrong move before they declare he's not a god. Then this whole nicey-nice act of theirs will crumble like a house of cards.

"Kirokai." Even through the wooden walls, I hear the deference in their voices. Good. So'Lan is coming. My rising panic immediately stands down.

For a split second, the crazy thought flies through my brain that they've made him a deal. Offered to spare his life if he snuffs mine out. I shake my head to toss that thought out of my head. That's crazy. Right?

The door opens and I see So'Lan's unmistakable silhouette in the opening. He's backlit from the flickering light from the fire in the pit. There he is. Broad shoulders, narrow waist, and the mighty mane of a lion-god. At least the tribespeople got that right.

"Hurry!" So'Lan orders, wanting them to unlock my manacles. As soon as I'm free, he sweeps me into his arms, clutches me to his chest, and stalks to our hut.

When the door closes us in, he drops to one knee to inspect my ankles.

"Were your shackles too tight? Did they hurt you in other ways?"

It's dim in here, but I can see the anger burning in his blue eyes. Sometimes, he lets his fangs show when he's in good humor—or highly aroused. There's nothing happy or sexy about the flash of fang I see now. It's menacing.

"Fine," I say as I rub my wrists to work some feeling back into them.

He gently bats my hands away to get a good look. When he sees the red marks there, which I assume are due solely to me trying to work my way out of the cuffs, he chuffs angrily. Dipping his lion-like head, he licks the chafed areas.

What an unexpectedly primitive behavior. It's so sexy to feel his burred tongue travel my skin, it makes me shiver in arousal. When he looks up at me, his gaze locking with mine, I feel a sexual zing between my legs. It's so carnal, so raw, a picture arrows into my mind with the speed of a bullet train. I want that tongue on me. Now.

Then I remember I've already been the beneficiary of that sexy tongue. Someone has been left wanting all evening. He deserves release.

Less than an hour ago, I was afraid I was going to die. Now it means nothing. The fact we're prisoners and the male they think of as a god is not in their good graces—I push that to the back of my mind. That there are armed males on the other side of the door? It's not worthy of a second thought.

No, the only thought pulsing through my brain is that I want to get my mouth on his cock. No. Not that. My only thought is that I want to *pleasure* him. I want to return the bliss he bestowed on me before that bizarre spectacle around the firepit.

I reach to him, placing one finger under his softly furred chin. With the barest pressure, I lift my finger, in turn lifting him, as he follows my unspoken instructions until he's standing tall. My arm is almost fully extended, still pressing under his jawbone.

Our eyes meet. In the dim light of our hut, it's as if sparks fly between us. He chuffs.

I'm learning his moods. His growl means only one thing. Whether it's loud or soft, it's a warning, meant to menace. All his other sounds have layers of meaning. He has chuffs of impatience, chuffs of irritation, and probably some for other meanings.

This chuff? This is a chuff of desire.

"So'Sexy," I tell him as I hold his gaze with the force of an imaginary vise.

This time it's me who dips low. Those young tribeswomen have nothing on me. I've never thought of myself as a particularly graceful person, but as I slowly sink to the floor, I never let my gaze release his.

Partway down, I lean closer, letting my lips touch his golden fur. On my slow slide, I slip my tongue out and trace a path through his parted fur.

Warm velvet. I want to say it out loud. To pay homage, but my mouth is far too busy doing other things.

I trail lower, past ridged abs and down his flat male belly. Over a jutting hipbone that is one of the few telltale vestiges of his enforced starvation.

Those are thoughts for another day. I don't want to think of pain right now. Not his, not mine, definitely not ours—nor what's in our immediate future.

No, in this moment, the only thing I want to fill my thoughts is pleasure.

And the instrument of it is pulsing inches from my face.

The room is warm, and the light is scant. His scent wafts to my nose over the tang of the soil, and the lingering smells of the stew in the still-warm pot in the village center.

As I take a deep breath in, all I smell is So'Lan. It's a yummy, delicious male smell. There's nothing sweet or flowery here. It's all masculine musk. I want to scoop it up, taste it on my tongue.

There's a golden bead of pre-cum on his cock, waiting to delight my senses, but I'm feeling like a femme fatale. I want to tease him. I want to work my way closer to both our rewards.

My tongue burrows into the crease of his thigh. He lets out a pant-hiss at the intimacy of it and his knees bend a fraction of an inch. I nestle closer so my teeth can gain purchase in the same spot.

Jackpot! I managed to pull the softest groan from him. Go, Phoenix!

Licking downward, I want to suck one of his balls into my mouth, but immediately realize the folly of my ways. They're huge. I'll have to settle for the popsicle technique.

He grips my shoulders, his claws exposed just enough to prick me in a gentle warning. Then he shivers as I bathe one plump, lightly furred ball with the flat of my tongue, then flick it swiftly until those claws squeeze tight enough to dissuade me from continuing.

I pull away long enough to chide, "So'Impatient," then grab his hips and breathe on the root of his shaft.

There are just two people in the galaxy right now. Him and me. So'Lan and me and my breath. I have all the time in the world as I wait for him to show some sign that I'm getting to him. I just breathe, allowing the warm, humid breeze to grab his awareness.

It only takes a moment for him to show cracks in his godlike armor. First, the tips of his claws press the tiniest bit harder against my shoulder. Then, his panting takes on a different cadence, his exhalations coming out in louder gusts. Finally, his hips thrust, making little micro-movements as they press toward me. It's a silent scold, or maybe a plea, for me to touch him.

I wait until our gazes meet before I extend my tongue, making sure to point it gracefully. Only now do I press it on the bulging vein at the base of his cock. It's a beauty, that cock. Thick and tall and completely devoid of fur.

I follow the vein up his shaft, stopping before it gets to the crown, then slide back down again.

"Phoenix!" he scolds.

Why do I love that he's losing it? Maybe the fact that these people think he's a god, yet I have so much control over him. It's gone to my head.

Finally, I take pity on him. Rising higher on my knees, I lick the beads of pre-cum from his head, letting the taste burst on my tongue. It's tangy and masculine. I flick his little slit and his knees buckle.

He's chuffing and purring at the same time, and I can't tease him any longer. We're both going to lose it if I don't suck him into my mouth right this minute.

I take him down as far as I can, licking along the underside. Then I lift away and take him in again, this time allowing my tongue to bathe a path down a different trajectory.

Working him hard now, I bob on him as far as I can take, swirling my tongue, although it's a tight fit. My fist surrounds his base and is pumping in time with my head.

My nose brushes his furred belly, gathering little gusts of his masculine scent. My mouth is bathed in his taste. I glance up to see this mighty, golden male in a posture that screams only one thing. Bliss.

His maned head is tipped back, Adams' apple standing out in silhouette. His lips are parted, fangs flashing in the dim light. His tail is low to the ground, flicking in impatience. His body is perfection and I'm controlling it. Doling out his pleasure. I vow to give him more.

Quickening my pace and tightening my pressure, I forget my original goal of wanting him inside me. His breathing speeds up as he releases a little grunt every time my head travels as low as I can manage.

All of a sudden everything changes. He grabs my upper arms, pulls me off him, and lifts me off my feet.

"You're an evil female." He whispered those angry words without a hint of displeasure. "A tease. Two can play at that game," he says as he tosses me onto the bed.

He was so aroused, I assumed he'd slide that golden cock inside me as soon as his knees hit the mattress. But no, he's full of surprises.

He crouches at my feet, opens his mouth wide, and takes my ankle into his mouth, careful not to use his fangs to break the skin. He releases a low growl. It's not menacing, just enough to tell me the tables have turned. To warn me he's in charge.

While I was sucking his cock, I was so tuned in to providing pleasure I was barely aware of my body's response. Now, though, I can't ignore the arousal racing through me. My nipples are beaded into hard points. I'm dripping wet. My desperation to be filled is so sharp it can't be ignored.

His soft mane tickles, in harsh contrast to the slight sting of his fangs as he drags them up my leg. The feeling is dangerous, menacing. When he gets to my thigh, he has a mouthful of meat in his grip. He shakes his head the slightest bit. It grabs my attention. If he shook harder, he'd tear meat off the bone. Instead, it just reminds me of how powerful he is, and how much he's holding back.

My channel flutters in response.

Instead of completing his slow journey to my pussy, he retreats to my other ankle. This time, he travels up my leg with the burred flat of his leonine tongue. It's just raspy enough to command my full attention.

This is so sexy I have to hang on. I grab his velvet shoulders and lift my torso enough to watch this magnificent beast work his way up my body. So much raw power is leashed in his furred form. It's the sexiest thing I've ever seen.

"Fuck me," I say as I lay my head down. It's too much. Overwhelming. I can't keep watching. I just want to feel.

With my eyes shut, I follow his progress in my mind's eye. He's the star of the show. I'm the audience, silently rooting for him to reach the apex of my thighs.

I can't stay still any longer, even though the back of my mind knows that one wrong move and those sharp fangs could do actual damage. I'm not sure I care. I just want that tongue to lick me, to invade me.

"Please," I hear myself say, then realize I've been chanting it for a while.

He's there. He's shouldered his way between my thighs. His soft mane grazes against my pubic bone, his hot breath wafts across my clit.

My next, "Please," escapes in a deep, guttural syllable full of both yearning and command.

Then, as if in slow motion, the flat of his tongue lands between my legs. It's so long, it spans from my channel to my clit. It doesn't move, just covers me, claiming the territory. In one bold move, he swipes that warm, rough tongue upward in a slow, sensuous lick.

Just that lick, that one lick, was so sexy, so perfectly timed, so highly anticipated, that I come. My nails dig into his shoulders as I arch off the bed, moaning in ecstasy. I manage the first syllable of his name. "So, So, So," I say, over and over as I spasm in delight.

I fall back onto the bed, spent from just that one release, but So'Lan has other plans. He uses his tongue to bring me to the heights of pleasure over and over.

When my thighs have spasmed so many times they're quivering from overuse, I find the presence of mind to reach between us, grab his magnificent cock and pull him to my entrance.

"Now or never, lion-man," I say through clenched teeth. "I can't take much more."

I guess he heard from the tone of my voice that I was serious, or maybe he couldn't wait anymore, either.

"From behind?" he asks.

I realize these are the first words he's spoken since we started. I don't let him see the disappointment on my face as I roll to all fours. This was my favorite position during my slave days. It was easier to tolerate when I didn't have to see their faces. It was the only way I could find pleasure with Gant because I got his ugly face out of my line of sight and used my hand to bring myself to completion.

I would have liked to watch So'Lan's gorgeous face as he came undone in bliss, but how can I refuse a male who just made me climax more times than I can count?

He covers me from behind, his movements slower than I'd anticipated. He's been full to bursting since we began. I figured he'd be more than ready to slide into me. God knows, I'm wet enough to take him.

He's not just slow, he's tender as his fur glides along my skin, sensitizing me. He notches his cock against me, and still, he doesn't enter me.

Dipping his mouth to my ear, now after nothing but chuffs and purrs and sexy growls during the evening's entertainment. Now he begins to talk.

"You're a treasure, Phoenix."

Those words bring hot tears to my eyes. Sex has always been a thing to be endured. A disconnected physical dance that meant nothing. I wonder if he knows that. If he's forcing me, no, forcing both of us, to acknowledge this is more than the mating of flesh.

"This has been such a surprise. A connection. Can you feel it?" he husks into my ear.

I'm not exactly sure what he wants. Not on a mental level. But in my heart, I know exactly what he's saying. We've shared a bond since he almost shivered off that tree branch. We've worked together, shared our supplies and our thoughts, and although it's unspoken, we might die together if the tribe decides to punish us.

"Yes," I admit as I press back against him. "A connection."

"Is this okay?" he asks as he grabs my shoulder with his fangs. It feels sexy and dangerous, just as it did on my leg earlier. But there's something more. I get it now. It's his way of asking me to trust him. To let go with him.

Does he know what he's asking? What he's asking a woman who's been a slave, who was stolen from her planet at eighteen and only survived for this long by two things: by her wits and by never trusting another living soul? Captain Thantose and his crew got my respect and admiration because of their kind treatment and human mates. But trust? No. Does he know what it means for me to allow this? To trust?

I guess he does. His story is almost the same as mine.

"Yes." I say. Then, to give it more emphasis, I repeat, "Yes."

He tightens his grip just the slightest bit, just to acknowledge what's going on here. What's really at stake. This is nothing like what I've ever shared before.

He's not covering me from behind so I can pretend it's not happening. He's doing it so I can let myself go—fully and completely. And I won't be doing it alone, the feel of his fangs on me will be there to remind me he's here with me, that he's got me. He's literally got my back.

I sink deeper into my body and let go of any remaining resistance. And then his cock eases into me. Despite our serious interlude, I'm still drenched for him.

I know I'm not his first female. It's common knowledge they reward gladiators with females for their wins. I imagine they're quick couplings.

This is the opposite of a quick, meaningless hookup. His fangs force me to keep my attention on our connection as I focus on his entry. I feel everything happening both in my channel and between our souls.

He slides in slowly, with a groan and a purr. Did I think this position would be impersonal? Now I can't imagine anything more intimate. His maned head is next to mine, his arms surround me, his fingers of one hand interlace with mine on the bed.

And his cock is filling me, stretching me, owning me. That beautiful cock is impossibly thick as he takes me almost lazily. All the way in and all the way out, so slowly I could almost weep with the beauty of our coupling.

Every deliberate thrust is like a sentence or a paragraph or a novel of affection, desire, and appreciation. I want him to speed up, yet I want this to never end. I feel taken and cherished and... seen.

Neither of us are virgins, not by a longshot. But he's masterfully allowing us to feel like this is our first time. I've certainly never swum in these uncharted waters before. Not a coupling filled with tenderness and emotion.

He releases his mouth's grip, licks the area, then puts his lips to my ear and husks, "Touch yourself. Don't come until I tell you."

Although I've never considered myself an obedient person, I follow his instructions to the letter as his thrusts become wild. His tail wraps around my thigh to hold me in place as he pistons into me. He's full of noises, chuffing and grunting. When his strokes become impossibly faster, he snarls, "Come."

My fingers had been circling as I worked myself. Now I press harder and detonate with a keening cry of pleasure even as he growls with his own release. He jets into me, retreats, and pumps again with another wet ejaculation.

My orgasm isn't a quick burst of bliss like my earlier ones. This one circles through my body like a tornado. It gathers force, touches down with intense pleasure, then repeats over and over until my spasms slow, then stop.

I can't stay on all fours for another second. When I fall to the mattress in a quivering puddle of pleasure, he joins me. We're a sweaty heap of limbs. My skin is slick from his release and my own. His fur is sticky with our fluids.

He's so spent, so obviously still in his happy place, I chuckle low in my throat.

"What's funny?" he asks. It takes a moment for those gorgeous blue eyes to focus on my face. Normally I'd laugh, but he's already confused.

"Just happy."

His brow quirks low, then returns to normal as he thinks. "Happy. That's a new emotion. I think I'm happy, too."

## So'Lan

Happy? Is that what this is? I've never been in this place before. My body is calm. I couldn't force my limbs to move even if I wanted to. I weigh a million *dextans*. I came so hard I imagine I drained myself dry. That felt so good perhaps I'll never come again. Even as that thought flies through my mind, I know it for a lie. With Phoenix so close, with her arousal scent so heavy in the air, I'll be ready to go at it again in *minimas*.

But this feeling is so much more than sex. More than the combination of friction and lubrication. It's deeper and wider and all-consuming.

I'm locked in a hut with guards at the door. I'm encircled by a hundred tribesmen who, on a whim, could decide to separate my head from my body. Yet I have this female at my side. And that makes everything good.

I want to claim her. I know, I just claimed her physically, but I want to tell her she's mine. I want to see her agreement on her face, in her eyes.

Not now, though. Too soon. Bad timing.

I rearrange us, tuck her against me, then pull her impossibly tighter. I can't declare my emotions with my words, but I can hold her and touch her and announce in a thousand other ways that what just happened in this room was more than shoving my cock into a warm *xyzca*. So much more.

# Chapter Eight

**P**hoenix

"Have I mentioned how ridiculous this is?" I ask as I shimmy into the horrid Goodwill dress they gave me last night.

"Yes. This is the sixth time, actually."

"Don't be an ass," I grouse.

"By the way you acted last night," he says as he turns his naked butt toward me and shakes it, "I thought that was a good thing."

In the span of less than a week, So'Lan has gone from a roaring addicted jerk who was so grumpy his friends had to hold him at gunpoint, to a bawdy comedian shaking his ass to make me laugh.

I can't argue with him after we made love for hours last night. It's a little late to pretend I don't find his ass both adorable and sexy as hell.

"So'Annoying," is all I say.

He chuckles. Boy, getting laid has certainly turned his frown upside down.

"Even though you find it ridiculous, this is part of the bargain I made with the chief. I'm to meet with the chief's daughter, Zendaya, and spend the day with her. Tomorrow is the competition. If I win, I'll be released from the expectation to mate."

"You'll be released. That is, if you don't fall madly in love with her and beg her to be your female."

His relaxed expression tightens for a moment as his mouth opens to argue, then he shuts it. After spearing me with a serious look, he says, "You and I both know that's not going to happen."

My tummy squeezes in pleasure at that. He may not have declared his undying love, but that was as close as I've ever gotten to such a statement.

"And you get to spend the day with the tribe's most eligible warrior," he taunts.

This was the deal he worked out with the chief and priest last night when I was locked in the punishment hut. He smartly kept this information from me while we spent half the night pleasuring each other. If he'd told me, I would have been too busy pouting to enjoy the evening's entertainment.

I don't mention, nor do I want to think about, the contest. He said it wasn't worth talking about, which means it's totally worth talking about. I shake my head to push that thought out of my mind. He's a gladiator. They couldn't have cooked up anything that would be too taxing, could they?

**So'Lan**

Zendaya and I walked for an *hoara* to get to her favorite swimming hole. It surprised me when they allowed me to carry a spear. I guess the chief's concern for his daughter's safety outweighed his fear of giving me a weapon. She's armed, too.

The little golden totems I received as tribute last night depicted many animals that must be native to this asteroid. I imagine none of them are friendly. I'm glad we have weapons.

Our journey has been almost silent. I don't know what to say to her, especially since I'm supposed to be a god. I certainly can't talk about my life, my gladiator days, or what happened to me in the dungeon.

She's quiet, too. Perhaps she's awed by my status. What is one supposed to say to a god?

"Here we are," she says softly when we arrive at a watering hole. It's surrounded by forest on three sides and protected on one side by a bluff made of red soil.

She kneels at my feet to help me remove my loincloth. Does she realize how intimate this is? The only female I want in this position is Phoenix. As I wave her away, my mind quickly flashes me pictures of our couplings last night. The new feeling I've discovered—happiness— washes over me.

Zendaya pulls her dress over her head and dives in. Assuming it's safe, I jump in after her.

We swim for a while, then tread water. Her gaze skitters from mine whenever I look at her. She's as uncomfortable as I am.

"Are you eager to mate with me? Is this something you wish?" I blurt, wondering what it would be like to spend your whole childhood being groomed to mate a god you'll never meet.

"It is what every female of the tribe aspires to," she answers, avoiding my gaze.

"But you, Zendaya? This is what you want?"

She freezes, forgetting to tread water, and almost dips under the surface before she kicks herself higher.

"What do you want?" I press.

"I want you, great Kirokai," she says without eye contact or emotion.

"There are many females in the tribe." I'll try another tactic to get the truth from her. "If I were to choose another, how would you feel? Please tell me the truth."

This time, her gaze flicks to mine, though it's only for a moment.

"I would be relieved, oh Great One. For there is another who owns my heart."

The sweet, terrified female keeps her eyes downcast. She's probably fearing both her father's wrath and my own.

"That is fine. Someone else owns my heart too."

For the first time today, a small smile lights her face. We both breathe a sigh of relief. Now all I have to do is win tomorrow's contest. At least I don't have to worry about breaking anyone's heart.

**Phoenix**

I've been walking with Ebudan for about an hour. He's very serious about his mission. He was evidently told to not only keep me safe but to court me. He's on guard, holding his spear at the ready. The courting part? He's kind of a fail.

Really, can you blame him? What do we have in common? Earth? No. This asteroid? No. Space travel? No. Since I can understand him, yet have no expressive language, it's been a strain.

The only thing we discussed that we have in common are the crockagators, which are called *megastos* in his tongue.

Finally, he points up ahead to some red bluffs that overhang a small, round pool of water. Look who's here. So'Lan and Zendaya.

He watches them for a moment, every muscle in his body straining. I can't say I spend too much time observing his reaction. I'm more interested in what's going on with So'Lan.

He and the chief's daughter are in the middle of the pool, treading water. They look to be deep in conversation. A pang of jealousy jolts through me. I've never experienced this before. I have a feeling of possession, ownership.

Planting my feet more firmly on the ground, I order myself not to do what part of me desperately desires—to march over to them and tell that bitch he's mine.

It's an interesting emotion, this jealousy. I was with Gant and watched him shamelessly flirt with anything with a vagina on every planet and space station we stopped at. All those years, I never gave a rat's ass about it. If anything, I was relieved when he got his needs met elsewhere.

But watching So'Lan chatting with the young, nubile chief's daughter is making my stomach clench.

Perhaps I'm crazy, but when I glance at Ebudan, I could swear he's feeling the same way.

"We should check on them," he says with finality. "I want to make sure the Great Kirokai is safe."

I don't challenge his faulty logic. First, if the Great Kirokai is so great, he shouldn't need a young warrior's help. Second, it doesn't look like the two of them want to be interrupted. He'll get no argument from me, though. I'd love to interrupt the serious conversation my male is engaged in with a naked girl.

*My male?* I ask myself. Well, yeah.

Ebudan leads us far off to their left before we leave the cover of the trees to walk in their direction. We're moving quietly and not talking. If I didn't know better, I'd say we're sneaking up on them. I think Ebudan and I would both like to know what they're talking about.

We must be pretty good at stealth-mode, because they haven't noticed we're approaching and Zendaya's voice drifts to me as she says, "He's just such a kind male. He's a great hunter. He'd be a good provider. He's so good with his younger brothers, I know he'd make a good father. I—" She sees us.

Her eyes widen and her beautiful mouth pops open. She's so busted. It doesn't take me long to figure out who she was talking about.

Ebudan runs to the edge of the water and asks, "Were you talking about me?"

He's leaning forward so much it's a wonder he doesn't fall into the water.

When Zendaya nods shyly, his head darts to So'Lan. "But, you're supposed to…"

"My heart already belongs to someone else, too," So'Lan says solemnly. "Go ahead, swim with your female. I'll stand watch. Don't worry. I'll speak with the chief when we return to the village."

Easily lifting himself onto the shore, he grabs his spear and walks to my side. He's naked and dripping water as he stands in the brilliant sunshine. I can't tear my eyes off him. Who could see this masculine perfection and not label him a god? My mouth goes dry with desire as my teeth catch my bottom lip.

We just stare at each other. I even manage to look him straight in the eyes, although I keep wanting to dip my gaze below his waistline.

"So… Zendaya and Ebudan are a thing?" I ask.

"It seems all the young females in the tribe weren't waiting patiently for the Great Kirokai to return," he says with a wry smile.

"Lucky us. Do you think the chief will let this drop? He'll stop pushing you to mate with his daughter?"

"The chief? Yes. The priest? No. He kept making the contest harder as time slipped by. I think he wants me to lose. He's power-hungry. With a god in the village, why would they need a mere priest?"

I walk into his arms, surround him in a hug, and press my cheek against his damp, furred chest. His back is to the water, and he's still tightly clutching his spear. I feel safe for the first time since we arrived on this shitty asteroid.

I'm an odd person. Perhaps if I hadn't been abducted by aliens, I'd have a good working relationship with a therapist on Earth, because the moment one fear is demolished, my mind finds another fear to take its place.

Not only am I worried about the competition it appears they've stacked against So'Lan, but it hits me with the force of a thunderbolt that this might be my life forever. I might be stuck on this asteroid, living in a hut with So'Lan for the rest of my days. I guess that wouldn't be so terrible. I'll have my lion-guy. There will be safety in numbers.

Except they think So'Lan is a god. What will happen when they realize he's just a male? They have our laser weapons. At some point, they're going to figure out all you have to do is press a button and it will shoot. Then it will be obvious So'Lan is just a person with fancy weapons.

And boy, are they going to be pissed. They'll think he lied on purpose. They're not going to take it well when the charade is exposed. My hands feel so clammy I have to force myself to restrain from wiping them on So'Lan's fur. I'm terrified.

"What's wrong, Phoenix?"

I glance at the couple in the pool. They're so consumed with each other, I doubt they realize we're still here. They must be relieved knowing nothing is in the way of becoming mates.

I debate for a moment about telling So'Lan, but we're in this together. All my worries spill out about my fears that they'll want to kill him when they realize he's been lying.

**So'Lan**

I dip my head to kiss her, but she's so panicked she barely kisses me back. I hadn't realized this strong, capable female was so full of fear. She hides it well, but it swirls just beneath the surface.

I've had to face death so many times in the arena, I learned long ago how to push my fear down so far inside me I can't even recognize it anymore. I'll need to be more mindful now so I can protect the precious female in my arms.

"You're right. Let's think about how to deal with this. I wish there were a way off this asteroid. That would solve all our problems."

But I'm close to giving up on that. The emergency buoy hasn't brought rescue, and our ship is out of commission.

# Chapter Nine

**P** hoenix

I am so glad I didn't eat breakfast this morning because if I had, it would be on the forest floor by now.

The entire tribe is here, at the banks of the river. I'm not sure, but if I were a betting woman, I'd wager this is the same river we discovered on our first day here. The river with the crockagators.

So'Lan wasn't exaggerating when he said the priest considered him a threat and wanted him dead. This contest looks potentially deadly.

Why should So'Lan have to fight these random tribal males for the privilege of mating me? Of course, we both know he doesn't want to mate me, but we were trying to find a way out of his obligation to mate the chief's daughter.

And why pit a being they think is a god against mortals? Frankly, the whole thing doesn't even make sense.

It's too late now. We just have to push through this.

"Welcome to this competition," the chief announces. "Kirokai will show his prowess against our best males. If he wins every match, he will earn the right to the female of his choice, just as has been our custom for generations.

"First, he and Ballam will swim across the river filled with *megastos*. We have a team of archers on the banks who will keep the beasts from killing Ballam."

What? Ballam's tribesmen will keep him safe, but So'Lan is on his own? Dear God, how is this fair?

"Go," the priest shouts without giving the males time to ready themselves. No. I take that back. Ballam was ready.

He hits the water with a splash and is swimming before So'Lan leaps from the bank.

So'Lan has the advantage of height. He's also in peak shape. He's completely detoxed and has told me he's regained all the weight he lost in the underground dungeon.

Within seconds, he's pulled even with Ballan and a moment later, he's ahead. I'm no longer worried about him winning this match. But I'm still terrified of the *megastos*.

So'Lan is on the return leg of the trip when the water looks like it's beginning to boil. It's the beasts. It looks like dozens, maybe hundreds figured out there were two edible morsels in their water. They're closing fast.

I didn't think it was possible, but both males somehow dig deep enough to hurry their pace. The animals are coming from downstream, which is the side So'Lan is on. They're going to encounter him first, and no one is going to lift a finger to keep him safe.

He has maybe fifty more feet until he reaches the shore. Several of the beasts, maybe a dozen feet long, are going to reach him before he arrives at the bank.

I could lose So'Lan! Hot pangs of panic dart through my body. This, like my jealousy yesterday, serves to make it clear just how much I care about this male.

One of the *megastos* has his mouth open, unable to wait to take a bite out of So'Lan's flesh. I can't watch. It's too horrible! Although I want to close my eyes, I'm too terrified to blink.

Ebudan pulls his bowstring back, lets his arrow fly, and pierces the rough hide of the beast closest to So'Lan. Ebudan's actions must give permission to the other hunters in the tribe, because a flurry of arrows is now flying, protecting my male from the horrific creatures.

Running through the thick reeds at the riverbank, I lean over, arm outstretched, and am there right in time to help So'Lan climb out of the water safely with one of the creatures snapping inches from his heels.

Another flurry of arrows rains down on the beasts, none of whom have the balls to come after any of us who are waiting on dry land. Another male offers his hand to haul Ballan out of the shallows and up the bank.

So'Lan is panting from his efforts. When he sees my face, he must see the terror in my wide eyes.

"Close?" he asks.

"You'll never know how close," I say. I know he's a big, bad gladiator, but if he knew he had been less than a second from certain death out there, I think it would wreck his concentration.

"The next match," Ammu announces, "will be held in the treetops."

He describes a competition of using the vines to go hand over hand from point A to point B. He hasn't even given So'Lan time to catch his breath. This contest is rigged. I knew the priest didn't like So'Lan, but now I'm pretty sure he wants him dead.

Still, I know he can do this, so I allow my heart to slow as I watch the next match. So'Lan is pitted against a warrior who is fresh and ready to compete, while So'Lan's chest is still heaving as he leans over, his forearms on his thighs.

The two males take off, and it's clear So'Lan, although he wasn't raised on this asteroid, looks like he was born and bred to win this challenge.

The males are out of sight for a while, but when one emerges from the trees and heads for the tree where they started, the finish line, I'm relieved to see my male's golden fur several trees ahead of his competitor.

He hasn't even climbed down from the tree when Ammu announces the next trial.

"We will move to the Sacred Cave," Ammu says, his voice grave.

So'Lan approaches me and grabs my hand as the entire assembly follows the river toward the bluffs we were headed for when he was captured in that net.

He dips to kiss the top of my head. How he can pay attention to me when his life is at stake, I'll never know, but he squeezes my hand as we walk. By the time we arrive at the bluffs, he's caught his breath and looks ready for the next challenge.

"As a tribe, we are lucky to have been blessed with the sacred cave. Kirokai should remember this place, for it was he, when he visited us last, who rolled this boulder to cover the mouth of the cave.

"You do not have a competitor," Ammu looks provocatively at So'Lan. "Simply move the boulder out of the way to allow us inside."

Holy shit.

Boulder is right. The thing is taller than So'Lan and has clearly been here for centuries. Years of pounding rain have combined with the rock's weight to have literally cemented the thing into place. At least it looks that way to me.

I know So'Lan's got his strength back. He told me he had been on track to becoming a Pinnacle gladiator. To do that, he must be prodigiously strong. But to move this monster? I think this is going to be a fail.

"Let me remind you," Ammu says with a sneer. "Failure means death. Those were the conditions you agreed to."

Death? The blood drains from my face. So'Lan casts me a sheepish look. I knew the stakes were high, but I never knew his loss would result in the death penalty. Tears spring to my eyes. No mortal could move this rock. I wonder how Kirokai managed it, because one thing I know for certain, he wasn't a god.

I feel like weeping when I look at So'Lan, then gaze at the boulder, which is taller than him. It's so big and heavy.

Ammu is smirking. I'd like to wipe that smug look off his ugly green face.

Something changes in So'Lan's demeanor. He stands taller, his shoulders lift in pride, and he raises his arms. I've seen vids of gladiator matches. Not of his, mind you. I never watched anything that was to be fought to the death. But I've seen this stance. It's performed at the beginning of a match. Each gladiator raises his arms like this in a silent request for the audience to clap and cheer.

"Kirokai!" I shout, then chant, "Kir-o-kai, Kir-o-kai," in a cadence designed to have everyone join me.

Soon, everyone in the tribe, including the chief himself, is chanting the golden male's name. His arms are raised in a powerful stance. Even his tail is lifted, almost dancing along with the cheer.

It's amazing. I just watched him psych himself up for this task. Closing my eyes for just a few seconds, I pray this worked. The male will need superhuman strength to accomplish this challenge.

He approaches the boulder and inspects the ground all around it. I imagine he's looking for the best direction to push from.

Finally, he leans his shoulder against it, digs the balls of his feet into the ground, and pushes with all his might. We all watch as he pushes and heaves. His grunts can be heard all the way to the back of the crowd. He struggles with the terracotta colored boulder for long moments, but it hasn't budged an inch.

"Tell us again, Ammu," the chief shouts above the noise of the crowd, "what are the rules?"

"He must move the boulder enough for us to enter the sacred cave of our ancestors."

"Are there no other rules?" the chief asks.

He's getting at something, but I can't fathom what.

"No."

The chief leaves his spot at the front of the crowd, walks to the boulder, sets his staff on the ground, and places his shoulder to the huge rock.

The crowd goes silent for a moment. We are all watching the two leaders —the chief and the priest—vie for power in front of the tribe.

The chief and So'Lan struggle with the boulder for a few minutes, but make no headway. When Ebudan strides toward the pair, it breaks the invisible rope that held everyone back. Every able-bodied male in the tribe joins the males at the boulder. Using the blunt ends of their spears, the older ones chip away the packed soil and rock around the base of the monolith. The chief steps away so all the strong, young males can touch the rock.

Soon there are forty hands on that boulder. The males are all working together as the chief rhythmically calls out "Heave.'

The rock finally pulls free of the hardened soil. At first, it's an almost imperceptible movement, then it quickly rolls forward until the cave is fully exposed. I don't know what's more surprising, the chief's help, that of the warriors who risked the priest's obvious wrath, or the cheer that erupts from the onlookers when the interior of the cave is revealed.

So'Lan turns and grasps the forearm of each male with a word of praise and thanks, ending with the chief. Leaning forward, he touches his forehead to the brow of the chief as he clasps his arms. The chief beams with pride.

Facing them, he holds his arms out from his sides as if to embrace them all as he addresses them. "I could have moved that rock, but I held off as a test, hoping all of you would respond just as you did. You have pleased me with your courage, honor and generous spirit. Thank you."

Ammu has watched the display quietly. I assume he thought even with all the males in the tribe they wouldn't be able to move it. Now that the task is accomplished, he's so angry his nostrils are quivering, his hands are clenching, and his facial muscles are so tight he barely looks like himself.

"I believe the Great Kirokai has earned the right to choose his mate!" the chief says exultantly, one fist raised in the air. "Right Ammu?" He turns to the high priest with a triumphant smile on his face.

A short nod is all the seething shaman can manage.

More happened here than moving a rock. I think the chief just won the power play we all just observed.

The males all move to rejoin the rest of the tribe.

"Oh Great Kirokai, show us what you have hidden in your cave." The chief ends his petition with a flourishing sweep of his arm toward the large opening of the cave.

So'Lan enters and returns in a moment, holding aloft a book.

As the crowd gasps. Ammu says, "The tome of the ancestors."

These people don't have a written language. I've seen no writing anywhere in the village. I wonder what it says. If I were to bet, I'd guess it's in Ton'arr.

**So'Lan**

Just like after a gladiatorial fight, it's hard for me to settle down after the contest. The tribe had another feast in my honor tonight, but I turned it around, declaring the feast was to honor their open hearts and generous character.

I enthusiastically approved when they honored Phoenix with a ceremonial dance because I claimed her as my intended mate. When they asked, we said we would formally mate at a later date. I wonder how long they'll let us wait before we're pressured into a mating neither of us want.

Neither of us want? Is that true?

No. I'd be honored to have this female at my side for the rest of my life. Here or elsewhere, it wouldn't matter. All I would care about is that having her with me would be the answer to a dream I seldom allowed myself to nurture.

I saw her face when she helped yank me out of the water, and again when the priest announced my task was to move the boulder. She cares about me, too. She just needs more time to admit it to herself.

We've both bathed and are sitting in bed when I open the tome. I never learned the Ton'arr language. I was abducted young, before I went to school. Over the *annums*, I learned to read a bit of Universal, and got good enough during my convalescence to be proficient.

After my release from the dungeon, when I searched the Intergalactic Database, looking for my roots, I encountered enough about Ton'arr to know what my language looked like. That's the language this book is written in.

"You can't read it?" Phoenix asks.

"Not a word."

We puzzle over it for a while. Neither of us can decipher a word. We leaf through, page by page. When we're almost to the end of the document, the writing stops. It becomes a picture book, but it doesn't appear to be for children.

Phoenix gasps, then points.

"This is a manual for a space vessel," she says. "Look here, that's the hyperdrive. Here's the electrical harness." She stabs her finger on an intricate design. "I think that's a photon cannon."

She laughs, although I see nothing funny about a manual we can't read for a vessel we don't have.

"What are you laughing at?"

"An old joke. A little boy is taken to a huge stable and told to muck it out as punishment. Instead of being sad or angry, he's excited and attacks the task with enthusiasm. When asked about it, he says eagerly, 'With all this horse manure, there must be a horse in here somewhere!'"

She cocks her brow at me, waiting for me to catch her meaning. I still don't get it.

"With a spaceship manual, there must be a vessel around here somewhere," she says with a grin.

# Chapter Ten

**T**wo Weeks Later
**So'Lan**

It must be the height of summer, because it grows hotter every day. Although I'm sweating under the heat of the sun, the physical labor feels good. My detox from Synth is behind me, I'm back to a healthy weight, and if my ability to carry heavy tree trunks is any indication, I'm as strong as I used to be.

As able as I am, I couldn't have moved that rock on my own. As my hope diminished with each passing moment and my impending death became more inevitable, the chief stepping forward to help me was the most surprising, uplifting, and humbling moment of my life. When Ebudan came to join us, followed by so many of the young males of the tribe, that was the proudest moment. Better than any victory I earned in the arena.

Although I'd prefer to leave this asteroid, it appears the disaster buoy Phoenix deployed will not bring rescue. She and I are coming to terms with the fact this is to be our home.

The tribe still reveres me, which causes Phoenix no end of fear. Every day she shares her worries with me that when they realize who I really am, they will kill me or cast us out of their tribe.

When the colossal beasts of the forest roar in the middle of the night, it terrifies her. We've seen golden statues of them. She calls them Tee-Rexes. She says on her planet they were enormous and we could never survive alone if we're banished from the tribe.

We're surrounded by most of the tribe as they help Phoenix and me build our hut. The chief said the hut we were using is reserved for visiting members of friendly tribes, and Phoenix and I should have our own place.

I glance past the mated females who are holding their skirts almost to their hips as they stomp a mixture of dirt, dried leaves, and water. They're preparing it to fill in the chinks between the wooden walls of our new home. My heart squeezes when I catch a glimpse of Phoenix's face. She's pretending to be happy, but underneath her false smile, she's sad and worried.

My need to protect her and make her happy is strong. If there is something I can do to improve her life, I will. My affection for her grows more intense every day.

Ammu, the high priest, sidles over to me when I step back to look at the hut from a short distance. As much as I enjoy the chief's company, the priest makes me uncomfortable. Every time I catch him watching me, I see his lips snarl in anger.

I understand why. He was revered here as *annum* after *annum* he told stories of the Great Kirokai and what would happen when the god returned. He was Kirokai's representative.

Now, with the Great Kirokai living here in the flesh, Ammu's position is superfluous. Phoenix has mentioned on more than one occasion that even though his power play was thwarted at the sacred cave, I should be careful of him. I agree. If anyone has a reason to resent me, it's him.

"Your female doesn't look happy about the hut you're building. Not fancy enough for a god's mate?"

The way he says the word god makes it clear he knows my secret.

"She has family elsewhere," I lie. "She knows we'll fly away back to her people when the time is right."

"Fly away, Kirokai? How will you do that?"

I don't like his tone, nor where this conversation is going.

"There are secrets a god must keep," I scold.

He scoffs. "I know *everything*."

He pauses. Just leaves that comment hanging in the air. Is he waiting for me to reveal myself? That won't happen.

"I agree with your mate on one thing. I, too, would like you to fly away. Your mate and I would both like you to leave this place."

He waits for a response. All I do is glance at him and lift a brow.

"I have the means to help you," he says. This time he waits for me to enquire.

"How would a priest help a god?" I ask haughtily.

"A god wouldn't need my help. But a mortal might be grateful to be shown a flying vehicle."

I don't move a muscle, trying to give nothing away.

I guess the fact that I didn't strike him dead with some magical lightning bolt is a confirmation of my true identity, because he continues, more boldly this time.

"The true story has been handed down for generations from one high priest to the next on their deathbed. As he lay dying, my predecessor told me what was told to him. That a liar and cheat came to our world and pretended to be a god by using cheap magic tricks to fool us. After amassing his weight in the gold metal he treasured so much, he was about to leave when he was eaten by a *megasto*.

"The original priest proclaimed Kirokai's disappearance had been planned, and invented the story that he would return someday. That priest had eight sons and they hid the scroll inside the cave one night when the moon was a sliver and the soil was soft. If the story is true, they only had to move it the length of my forearm. The stories about the great Kirokai's return kept the tribe optimistic and productive and kept our females chaste. The priest gets his choice of virgins when he wishes a mate." He smirks.

All the virgins he wants *and* it kept the priest class in power. Very clever.

"I imagine every priest before me did what I did. After hearing the story, they explored where the vessel was hidden to see if the tale was true. I've seen it with my own eyes, pressed all the buttons.

"The story says it hums when it is activated, but it made no noise for me. Perhaps you know how to turn it on." He pauses and waits for our gazes to meet, then adds, "No one wants you gone more than me, *Great One*.

You've gotten a taste of it these last weeks. It feels good to be revered, no? I will keep your secret and help you leave. If that doesn't happen…"

When he cuts his gaze toward me, it reveals his true nature. He might hide behind his priestly exterior, but this is no holy male. He is power-hungry. When he continues, the lengths to which he will go to stay in power become even more clear.

"I will keep your secret. I will show you the vessel. Before you leave, you must do something for me. You must promise to return from where you came and never come back, leaving me in charge. Only me. And…" he pauses for effect. "You must kill the chief."

I don't give my answer much thought. I don't believe his story. A spacegoing vessel that's been hidden on this asteroid for hundreds of *annums*? And even if that's true, how could it still be in working order?

This male is a liar. If his words are true, I'll figure out how to wiggle out of my promise later. The last thing I would want to do is kill the chief and leave this *dracker* in charge of such a good tribe of people.

**Phoenix**

So'Lan has been distant all day. Well, not all day, just since Ammu ambushed him right after lunch. I don't worry about what's wrong. I'm beginning to trust my lion-man. If there's something I need to know, he'll tell me. Trust. Hah, I'm learning a new skill.

Another new skill? I'm learning the native language quickly. And I'm getting the hang of this whole bathing with one bucket of water thing. We stand in a little indent in the hard-packed soil that was built for this purpose and use one bucket each to wash the dirt off.

I imagine I could do fine by myself, but it's so much more fun for me to wash him—and for him to wash me. I like to do him first, because by the time he's done washing me, I'm ready for him to join me in bed.

"We'll have our own hut soon," I say, then give a little giggle. Life sure has a way of throwing me curveballs. A year ago, I wouldn't have been able to imagine those words coming out of my mouth, or that they would bring me a modicum of happiness.

"Aye," he says as he turns me toward the wall so he can wash my back. He's a multi-tasker. While he washes me, he licks that sensitive spot on my neck. My nostrils quiver as I quit worrying about my life and future and focus only on how my channel clenches in need for him.

He nips me with those deadly fangs, making sure to do it just hard enough to turn me on. He breathes a warm stream of air right under my ear, which makes me weak in the knees.

"We need to talk," he says seriously as he takes a step back.

Shit. I knew it.

"Ammu?" I ask, suddenly all business, as I turn to watch his expression.

Ten minutes later, we're both clean, tucked into bed, and sex is the last thing on our minds.

"I knew it! There had to be a vessel to go with the manual. But, do you believe him?" I ask. "Do we dare trust him?"

"We'll find out at dawn. He's taking us there."

# Chapter Eleven

**S** o'Lan

It occurs to me that Ammu might be leading Phoenix and me away from the village so he can kill us. I'm sure there are warriors loyal to him who could be hiding in the jungle, ready to follow his instructions. I'm doubly wary because he didn't protest when both Phoenix and I arrived carrying spears.

She and I discussed it and decided if he wants us dead, he can easily accomplish it anytime, anyplace. We might as well see if he was telling the truth and if there's a vessel hidden out here somewhere.

We pass through a thick part of the forest, where the trees are so numerous we can barely see the sky through the overhanging leaves. Up ahead, almost hidden by the trees, is a bluff with a wide gap that opens to a cave.

I'm on guard, every muscle in my body ready to fight. If he has less than ten tribesmen here to do his bidding, I believe Phoenix and I will be safe. Between my fangs and claws and my experience in the arena, I can take them all. I'll just be beside myself, worrying about my female while I fight them.

Much to my surprise, there are no tribesmen. It's just the priest and us.

Although it takes a moment for our eyes to adjust, it's immediately apparent Ammu told the truth. There's a metallic vessel lurking in the dark depths of the cave.

We build a fire at the mouth of the cave and carry torches inside to inspect it. I'm a gladiator. I know a hundred ways to kill. I know nothing about space vessels. I await Phoenix's assessment.

"This is an old one, all right," she says as she circles the ship. "Older than anything I've ever worked on."

She climbs inside and looks around. After a moment, I don't see her head as she leans down. She must be inspecting things under the nav screen.

"The odds of this thing being able to lift off or travel through space? I'd say close to zero," she calls from inside the ship. "I didn't expect her to turn on. She's been sitting here for hundreds of years, but there are a thousand things that could be broken."

She climbs out and opens a panel in the exterior.

"I have to say, it's not in as bad a shape as I'd imagined. Just think of all the parts that could have developed dry-rot, or might have been carried off by animals. I'm surprised there aren't animal nests in the wiring."

She turns to Ammu. "I'm going to be working on her. I'll come out here every day to see what I can do. Is this acceptable?"

"As I explained to…" he pauses, gesturing, but not wanting to call me Kirokai, "this must remain a secret."

"Absolutely. We all want the same thing—get us off this planet and leave you in charge. Got it."

"One more thing," he says as he faces Phoenix, but glances at me out of the corner of his eye. "Is there one part you must have to make this thing fly?"

"They're all important."

Does he think it goes by magic? Perhaps he does.

"One piece that if you removed it would make the vehicle useless?"

"Well, the crystal thruster control," she says with a shrug.

"I want to have it." He holds his hand out, palm up.

"Why did you bring us here if you aren't going to let us leave?" she asks.

"You work on this machine. I'll give you the crystal thruster control *after* you've killed the chief."

*Drack*! Phoenix and I hadn't quite figured out how we were going to deal with his demand we kill the chief, but I figured it would involve us taking off in the middle of the night. I guess that can't happen now.

"I'll leave you here," he says as he turns toward the forest, ruby-colored crystal in hand.

"I considered giving him the spaceship equivalent of a gearshift knob," Phoenix says when he's deep in the forest, "but I stupidly mentioned a crystal. There was only one on the ship."

"We'll figure something out," I say, although I don't have a clue how we're going to get out of this.

She's already turned back toward the vessel, her arms hugging her waist, her head cocked to one side.

"This will take some time," she says as she replaces the panel she opened on the exterior of the ship. "I'm going to have to inspect every inch of wiring, make sure everything is as it should be. There will certainly be no spare parts at the ready." She gives a rueful laugh and shrugs.

"You can do this on your own? I won't be able to help."

"I'd say the odds are close to zero I can get this baby to fly. I'm not the greatest mech. I mean sure, Gant's ship was a piece of crap, and near the end I was completely in charge of repairing it, but I'm no expert."

I assumed Phoenix had a difficult life. She comes across as harder than most of the other Earther females I've met. We had an odd beginning to our relationship, starting off as more enemies than friends.

Since then, I've detoxed, we've had to fit into a tribe of natives, and we've been very busy in bed—and up against the wall. I've been looking for an opening to ask her about her past. She just gave it to me.

"I've been waiting to ask, Phoenix, but is now the time to tell me about… Gant?"

She stills, almost paralyzed as she considers my request, then shrugs.

"It's not pretty. Are you sure you want to hear?" Her gaze flinches from mine when she cocks her head in question.

Phoenix is such a strong female. I picture her ordering me to move my ass within moments of the crash. It always surprises me when she presents as anything other than a force of nature. She's uncertain I will accept her if she tells me her history?

"I know who you are, Phoenix. I've already formed my opinions about you." I let my affection shine through my eyes. "You're fierce, capable, compassionate, and intelligent. Do I have to mention that I think you're the prettiest female not only on this asteroid but in the entire sector? I would think my feelings on that were obvious."

I trace my knuckles gently down her cheek, then bend to kiss her there.

"Nothing you tell me will change that. I care about you. I want to know what makes you you. But don't tell me if it will make you uncomfortable."

She grips my hand and pulls me into the vessel's nav seat, then walks around to sit in the pilot's seat. It's musty in here, but it's been watertight. I don't see evidence of animal life in the craft. I noticed what looked to be nesting material in the back of the cave but can't determine how recently it's been used. No evidence of occupancy now.

She keeps her eyes straight ahead, as if she's steering us among the stars. I follow her lead and do the same, keeping my face immobile as she tells me everything that's happened to her over the last decade. She doesn't want my pity, so I won't show it to her. Instead, I tuck my hands under my thighs and allow them to clench and unclench as she shares everything from the moment the slavers stole her from her bed on Earth.

My stomach rolls when she tells me about her time in a brothel. It's a miracle this female can take any pleasure from our bed-play. I know I shouldn't, but I take pride that despite her history, she can enjoy what we share in bed. In the beginning, I'd intuitively let her take the lead.

Perhaps that's what helped her find safety in my embrace. Lately, it's allowed me to take a more dominant role in our coupling.

I admit, I felt a bit of jealousy when she first mentioned Gant by name. As soon as she described how they met, and how he treated her for the *annums* they were together, my envy disappeared. How can I envy a male she hated?

Halfway through her story, she reached out to pat my leg. I immediately grabbed her hand and have been drawing soft, slow figure-eights on her palm with my thumb.

She's come to the end of her story, and I can feel her looking at me. Turning in my seat, I give her the full force of my gaze.

"You've been a surprise," I say, knowing she needs to hear I'm not disgusted by her tale. I want to give her so much more than feeble reassurances. "I'll admit. I didn't have a positive opinion the first time we met. That might have something to do with the fact that I was in the throes of withdrawal and you were looking at me like I was an insect you wanted to squash."

I give her a tight smile, but she's still waiting for my pronouncement. I hurry to continue.

"But after our initial meeting, I have nothing but respect for you. I've killed males. You must know this. I was a gladiator. I'll make no excuses for it. We do what we must when our lives are not our own."

I raise her chin with my knuckle. After turning her head toward me, I wait for her to gaze into my eyes.

"I'm honored to be with you, Phoenix. I care for you. Nothing you've done while you were a slave can change that."

She smiles for the first time since we entered the vessel.

"And my profession? Being a pirate?" she asks with a toss of her head.

"It's sexy," I breathe as I close the distance to kiss her.

After a moment, she breaks the kiss. "I want to get off this asteroid, Your Highness. Let's finish this back in the hut. I want to get to work. But first, I should tell you about my name. I gave it to myself."

My chest fills with pride as she tells me the story of the phoenix rising from the ashes. It's an inspiring tale of redemption and rebirth. I especially like that she gave it to herself as a fresh beginning after she left Gant and began a new life on the *Serenity.*

**Phoenix**

"Your work here is done," I tell So'Lan around lunchtime. "I brought some jerky Ebudan gave me. You've cleaned everything there is to clean, and there's nothing more you can do. I'll be back at the village in a few hours."

He argues for a minute, but he's useless now that the cleaning is done. "I'll come for you. I don't want you walking in the forest alone." At first, I'm reluctant, wanting to argue, but he's right. All I have to do is remember the hundreds of crockagators before I agree and give him a lingering kiss before he exits the cave.

It's only when he's completely out of sight that I take a deep breath and examine what's going on inside me. I never thought I'd share my story with anyone. Certainly not a male I was sleeping with.

The men I was with on Earth would have been repulsed. Well, maybe that's harsh. Maybe *I'm* the one who's repulsed. My face heats with embarrassment, then unwelcome tears begin to fall.

Of course I'm disgusted. The experience was horrendous. But telling it, vomiting it out to someone who accepted me unconditionally, was cathartic.

What a ridiculous moment. One second I'm crying, and now I'm smiling through my tears. There's something about telling So'Lan, feeling his warm grip urging me on even while he looked at a blank screen so I didn't feel examined or judged, that freed a part of me that was stuck in the past.

I take a deep breath and get to work. I'm starting with the nav harness. I'm going to trace every wire in this vessel to check its connections. Tomorrow, I'll inspect the thrusters. One step at a time before I even try to turn this baby on.

An hour later, the hairs on the back of my neck stand on edge. I'm not stupid. I've kept my spear handy no matter where on the vessel I've been working. I grab the spear as I turn, fully expecting to see a contingent of warriors sent by Ammu.

Instead, I see a troop of scarlet and cobalt monkey-like animals streaming through the mouth of the cave. They're half adorable, half creepy, with their big-eyed monkey faces and their six spider-like legs.

Their cute faces aren't lulling me into complacency, though. I'm still clutching my spear as I assess how to stay alive if they all attack at once. There's maybe a dozen of them of various sizes. I think I just met the critters who've been using this cave as a home.

They're chittering and squawking as they continue to invade my space. Now that they've formed a semi-circle around me, I decide they're definitely not friendly. They're not keen on visitors. They're in attack mode.

I'm not going to wait to see what they do. I need to be on the offensive. "Shoo, shoo, get the fuck out," I yell as I brandish my spear at them.

One of the smaller ones who had been at the front of the line skitters to the rear, but the others hold their ground.

My back is to the ship. The creatures can only approach from the front. That's good.

Although I've been practicing each day with So'Lan, learning the finer points of spear throwing, I can't use my weapon for its intended purpose. Once thrown, I'll be defenseless. No, I can only use it as a stabbing implement.

Their shrieky babble increases, and all at once they rush me. I'm not a fighter, I'm a pirate. I force down my panic as my hands tighten on the spear's shaft.

I just keep stabbing as they approach. Luckily, the hands on their four arms are long, thin, and don't have claws. Their fangs are more like human canines than So'Lan's lion-like fangs. They wouldn't be deadly if they weren't attacking me in a menacing pack.

I lunge, stab, and retreat until my back hits the vessel's hull. I continue: lunge, stab, and retreat. Now that I've killed some and injured a few others, their shrieks have risen a million decibels, the cacophony reverberating crazily through the stone cavern.

One of them gets smart, makes an end-run around the vessel, climbs on top of it, and jumps on me from above. He bites into my shoulder. Although his teeth aren't much sharper than my own, his jaws must be a million times more powerful. I choke up on my spear, cross it over my body, and jab at the thing until I pierce its throat.

Flinging the dead body at the remaining creatures, I scream at them, then approach menacingly. Perhaps it was being pelted with their comrade's dead body, but the five remaining creatures run off hooting and screeching.

Glancing at my left shoulder, I see my clothes are soaked with blood and it's still pouring out of the wound. Shit. There are other critters in the jungle. I'm sure they can all smell an injured animal.

I close the doors to the vessel, clutch my spear tighter, and take off at a run.

What the hell was I thinking? I should have just retreated into the vessel and locked myself in. So'Lan would have come looking for me eventually. He could have dispatched all twelve with one hand tied behind his back. I've been independent for too long. Having someone who'll look out for me is still too new for me.

My heart is pounding, and the area where that fucking animal bit me is on fire. I can't wait for So'Lan's return. I have to return to the village.

Luckily, I paid attention on the way here, so I set off toward the village at a jog. Keeping my guard up the whole way, I try to pay attention to the jungle noises and stay on guard for crockagators and monkey things, and any number of other creepy asteroid animals.

"I fucking hate it here," I whisper when I break into a dead run.

# Chapter Twelve

**S** o'Lan

Excited shouting breaks my concentration as I'm laying the skeleton of sapling trunks across the top of what's going to be the hut I'll share with Phoenix. Climbing down from the crude ladder, I break into a run when I catch their voices on the wind.

"Hurt… bleeding."

There's no doubt in my mind those words are describing my Phoenix. I've heard of people's hearts seizing in their chests, the convulsion killing them in one strike of the clock. For a moment, I wonder if this is what's happening to me as I struggle to draw breath.

No. This pain, this inability to breathe, has nothing to do with my body. It's hurting my soul.

I see two warriors approaching the village, running as fast as their legs can carry them. One is clutching my female to his chest.

I run to him and heft her into my arms without missing a step. It's as if that young male and I had practiced for *lunars* passing a baton in a footrace.

I bring her to Ba'Rell's hut, calling at his doorway. The chief's wife, the tribe's healer, welcomes me inside.

Phoenix is unconscious. One warrior says she passed out in his arms a few moments after he and his friend found her staggering and weakly calling my name in the forest. He said she spoke the word, "Mun-kees," then closed her eyes and went limp.

"Mun-kees?" Celletta, the chief's wife, asks, shaking her head. "Looks like a *preniten* bite."

Celletta treats Phoenix until well after sunset. She throws special leaves on the coals in the center of her hut. She says they have healing properties and will help fight infections. Then she cleans Phoenix's wounds and sews closed a deep gash.

When Ba'Rell encourages me to leave and get some food, I shake my head. At some point, I sagged to the compacted soil floor and leaned against the hut wall as I continued to watch.

Phoenix is naturally pale, but she's even more ashen now. She's so small and slim, if I didn't know her I'd think she'd be meek. But this female is strong and courageous. I've come to believe she can do anything. Is that why I was foolish enough to return to the village when she urged me to?

I'll never forgive myself for leaving her alone in that cave. Did I learn nothing from my encounters with the vicious *megastos*? This asteroid isn't a safe place.

I vow to myself I'll never leave her alone again. But in order to do that, she must live.

Our couplings have been more than physically fulfilling. They've touched emotions I long ago ceased believing I'd ever find. I've known, though, since that first night in the hut, that our connection went far deeper than a sexual mating. I've just doubted it, denied it to myself, and I've never admitted it to her.

Yes, earlier today when she told me her story, I let her see glimpses of my deep feelings for her, but I was too cowardly to say them out loud. If she awakens, not only will I never leave her alone again, I vow I will express how I feel.

My body slumps in misery when I think she might even now be on her journey to the afterlife without knowing my true affection for her.

Several of the males at Sanctuary have mated Earther females. I've been to their mating rituals. I've heard them pledge their love to each other. I said nothing, but inside my mind, I scoffed. Love is such a childish word. It's cheap. It signifies nothing.

Now, though, when I replay those ceremonies in my mind, I see how happy that word made the females, and how earnest was the look on the males' faces when they pledged it.

If my female wants to hear that word, I will say it to her morning and night.

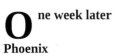

**O**ne week later
**Phoenix**

"I'm glad you're coming with me," I tell So'Lan as he accompanies me to the cave. The first day back, So'Lan made me wait outside the cave with my spear ready while he went in to make sure no *prenitens* were in residence.

We then cleaned out all the nesting material. It didn't look like they had returned, and all the ones I killed were also gone. Did they come back for their dead or did another animal take advantage of the ready meal? Not sure I want to know.

It's usually pitch dark farther back in the cave. Perhaps it's the time of day or the angle of the sun, but something catches my eye.

I grab my spear in one hand and So'Lan's wrist in the other and pull him deeper than we've ever explored. It's so dim it takes a moment to discern what I'm seeing. We both come to the same conclusion at the same time. A body.

It's humanoid, and by the four canines still remaining in his jaw, it's clearly a Ton'arr.

"Kirokai," I whisper.

"Aye," So'Lan agrees.

"Ammu said he was killed by a *megasto*, which would place him near the river. My money is on the priest," I say.

"We'll never know, but I think you're right. When the original Kirokai threatened to leave, not magically, but in his spaceship, it would have removed all the priest's power. He couldn't let the male escape."

"Kirokai was a greedy bastard," I say, "but…" My eyes are more accustomed to the dark and as I edge closer, I see his skull was bashed in. "But he didn't deserve this."

We stand in silence for a moment. "Ammu might be about to double-cross us, too." So'Lan says, "I don't think so. I think he just wants us gone. If he were going to kill us, he would have done it already."

We walk to the vessel and as I get to work I ask, "What's our cover story? It's the third day in a row we'll be gone all day."

"That we are preparing for our mating ceremony and it requires our spirits to commune for *hoaras* each day in the privacy of nature."

"Not bad, So'Smart," I say as I tap my temple.

"Do you want me to carry you?" His tone is so eager, so un-So'Lan-like. He's been like a different person since I woke up from my coma five days ago.

"I didn't want you to carry me two days ago, or yesterday. Nor do I want you to carry me today. I'm better."

"What I told the chief wasn't so far from the truth," he says. "We *should* be communing in the privacy of nature as we prepare for a mating ceremony. I will ask you again if you will be my mate. It would make me the happiest male in the galaxy."

So'Lan has been a mess since I tangled with those monkeys. Or, well, since they tangled with me. I must have been close to death, because he's not the same male he was the day of the monkey attack.

I know he means well, but he's smothering me. I get it. I agreed he should be with me on my jaunts to the vessel. It's obvious I need protection. But he wants us to mate. That's not on my agenda.

Fucking? Yes. Affection? Yes. And hey, if we can't get this metal bird in the air and we're doomed to stay on this rock forever, I'll enthusiastically endorse living together in the primitive hut we're building. But I'll never mate. Especially not a Synth addict. Even a *former* Synth addict. I watched Gant try to quit a dozen times. It never took.

There's alcohol here, and something like marijuana that Celletta uses. She gave me some for the pain—it's potent. With alcohol and drugs freely available, where there's a will, there's a way.

"I think today's the day," I tell him, totally ignoring his mating proposal. Whoops! With the elated look on his leonine face, he thinks I just accepted his proposal. I quickly amend, "The day we'll see if this baby can fly."

Shit, he looks like I just drowned his favorite puppy. I stop walking and step into his space. His arms automatically embrace me as he lifts me higher so I can be face to face with him.

"I love you, Phoenix. I love your brave heart and your courage and your strength. Seeing you so close to death almost broke me. *I've* been near death a dozen times in my career as a gladiator. In that black dungeon of despair, I wanted to die, but any attempt to end our lives by refusing to eat or drink the meager rations resulted in everyone getting flogged. None of us could tolerate being responsible for the increased suffering of a brother gladiator.

"Seeing *you* ill? It gutted me." He kisses my forehead. "I'll stop asking you to mate me. Every morning when the sun rises, just remember the sun is rising as a reminder that I want to be your mate. Every night when you see the moon, it too should make you remember the offer is open.

"I won't ask again personally. The sun and moon will do it for me. When you're ready, though, *you* will have to ask *me*."

"So'Sweet." I kiss him on the lips. Hoping my actions tell him how much I care for him. I'll never be able to say "I love you" out loud to anyone. Even the best male I've ever met. Too bad he has a fatal flaw.

It's after midday when I have So'Handy tighten the final screw. I wipe my palms on my leather pants. They're designed to take a beating, but after the last few weeks, they're filthy. The thought that I'll still be wearing them when they're in shreds twenty years from now if we're still on this primitive asteroid, well, it makes me cringe.

After So'Lan won the contest and Ba'Rell acknowledged me as the Great Kirokai's intended mate, they provided me with many colorful sleeveless tunics that reach below the knees. It's what the women of the tribe wear. I still prefer my leather pants with a short tunic on top. It's too hot for my vest.

"I think I've done everything I can do," I tell him. "To think I've worked on an antique vessel with a less-than-helpful user's manual, no spare parts, and not even a wrench? It's either a miracle or a delusion. If we get her in the air, I'll deserve a medal."

"You deserve a medal either way," he says. Wow, when he looks at me like that, with his blue eyes shining with affection, it almost makes me want to say yes to his mating proposal. Almost, but not quite.

"I won't know if she'll really fire up until we have the crystal. We're as close as we're going to get, though. Now we have to discuss the whole kill-the-chief thing."

"I've been thinking about how to do it…" he says thoughtfully. Five minutes later, he finishes with, "You don't look well. Are you having a relapse?"

# Chapter Thirteen

**P**hoenix

I'm in So'Lan's arms, possibly in shock, when he carries me from the chief's hut to our own. It's many hours after sunset. The village is quiet. The full moon is high overhead.

I feel horrible about what we just did. I'll never get the scene out of my mind. Dear God, it was a bloodbath in there. I shudder, picturing the scene we just left—Ba'Rell and his mate, Celletta, bathed in blood.

Ammu knocks as soon as So'Lan sets me gently on our bed.

"I saw you leave the Ba'Rell's hut. Is it done? Are you ready?" he demands without preamble.

So'Lan tosses me a wet rag to wipe the blood off my face and hands. It sprayed everywhere. He's also cleaning himself as he speaks to the priest in low tones.

"Keep your voice down," he scolds Ammu. "We're packed, ready to go. We'll need the crystal. We need to move! Now! Before anyone knocks on the chief's hut and sees what we've done."

"How do I know I can trust you?" Ammu asks as he squints at So'Lan.

"Go look, but be quick. We must move fast or we're all dead. Phoenix and I won't take responsibility without dragging you down with us. It's in your best interests to get us off this asteroid."

Two minutes later, I've shucked my blood-slicked leathers and pulled on my colorful tribal dress. When Ammu returns, his face is a lighter shade of green than before.

So'Lan clasps my hand, and we sneak through the darkness and slip into the forest.

We walk as fast as we can, considering the leaves above are so thick only thin shards of moonlight slip through to light our path. My stomach is in a knot. I'm terrified. There are so many working parts to this. Mainly because we don't know if the ship will fly.

Again, the picture of the mess we left in the chief's hut invades my mind. Will I ever be able to erase it?

We finally arrive at the cave. I've been terrified of a thousand things going wrong. I imagined the monkeys raided the ship and tore everything apart. I wonder if this old bucket of bolts will work. I worry that our whole plan will fall down like a house of cards and we'll not only be stuck on this asteroid, but half the tribe will hate us for what we've done.

Ammu came with two warriors loyal to him. They're here for protection, but we use them to help push the small ship out of the cave and into the clearing. If the ignition works and I get this baby flying, I'm going to have to shear off the tops of some trees to get off the ground.

I walk around the vessel, opening the exterior panels to ensure nothing was tampered with. Then I crawl inside and check all the wiring harnesses. When I'm certain it all looks like it did when I left, I stick my hand out the door, palm up.

"I need the crystal," I say, putting steel into my voice, although I'm not feeling confident at all.

So'Lan has been standing outside the hatch, waiting for me to complete my pre-flight check. He lowers his spear and points it at Ammu's heart. In turn, the two warriors aim their spears at So'Lan.

"Hold," commands So'Lan. "I may not be a god, but I am a warrior with far superior reflexes. Your high priest will have his heart impaled before either of you can blink and both of you will be next." He lances Ammu with his most terrifying look and threatens, "Don't even think of double-crossing us. Hand her the crystal and have your warriors drop their spears, then back up to the edge of the forest."

Ammu scowls, his eyes blazing with hatred as he nods his head at his warriors. They hesitate a moment, but when the tip of the spear in So'Lan's hands presses against Ammu's robe-covered chest, they drop their weapons and move away.

My stomach calms when I feel the weight of the ruby-colored crystal in my palm after So'Brave eases into the nav seat and latches the hatch.

It's tiny in here, barely enough room for the two of us, with a small bed in the back.

"So'Lan, there's no reason for both of us to die. I guess we should have talked about this earlier, but do you think I should take her up for a test run without you? If it explodes, or loses power and crashes back to the ground, only one of us would be lost."

We've been moving so fast since the bloodbath in the chief's hut, I haven't spared a moment to really consider the repercussions of our actions. I haven't given myself a second to experience my emotions. It would be too terrifying. If things don't go according to plan, we're going to die.

Now, though, So'Lan grabs my hand in his and waits until I give him my full attention.

"We're in this together, my love. I wouldn't want to stay here without you." He bends his beautiful face, surrounded by that fierce chestnut mane, and presses a hard kiss to my lips. It's less a kiss and more like he's sealing a deal.

"Take her up," he orders.

I look around, imagining a tribe full of natives with torches and spears are even now making their way through the forest.

My eyes aren't playing tricks on me. "Torches!" I say when I see flashes of light wending their way through the trees.

I install the crystal and hit the power button.

Nothing.

Shit. Terror flares through me. The ignition didn't even flare for a moment. The machine is dead!

I press the power button again. Nothing.

"No, no, no," I moan. "I wasn't sure this thing would fly, but I had no doubt it would start." I mentally review everything I did. Every nut and bolt I had So'Lan tighten. Every inch of wiring I ensured was intact and properly connected. There's no reason we shouldn't at least hear the hum of the vessel coming to life.

It's the middle of the night. We're out of the cave, but it's almost pitch black in the cabin. For me to troubleshoot, I need more light. I glance out the window and see the torches approaching. They're bouncing. The people carrying them are at a run. My stomach squeezes in fear. If we don't leave right this minute, there's going to be a terrible confrontation. I don't want to be here for it.

"What's that?" So'Lan asks as he points to the starter button.

"The starter button," I answer irritably. He admitted himself, he's no mechanic. Now's not the time to distract me.

"No, that." He points again.

"I don't see anything."

"This little hole in the button."

I hadn't even noticed it before, but there's a little hole in the center of the red ignition button. I shrug. It means nothing to me.

"What if it's a failsafe against theft?" he asks. "Rather than using a fingerprint reader, what if it ensures only a Ton'arr can pilot this craft?"

Well, he's right about one thing. This was definitely a Ton'arr ship. It had to belong to the lion-man who came before. The one whose image is carved onto the surface of half the trees in the area.

"I think it's meant for a claw," he says as he bares his sharp, curved claws.

Just as he's about to slip a claw into the hole in the button, shouting breaks out behind us.

It looks like every adult in the tribe is surrounding our ship. I don't think we can go anywhere. If So'Lan is right and the engine starts with his claw, the thrusters will end up hurting many of the males we've come to like and respect. I had wanted to avoid this. It's going to be ugly.

The chief, with every warrior in the tribe at his back, approaches Ammu and places the tip of his spear at the male's throat. He's still bathed in blood from our little charade, as is Celletta who is at his side.

"You tried to have me killed," the normally calm chief seethes through clenched teeth.

"It was them," Ammu accuses as he points at us. "Kirokai used his powers to put me into a dream state. He forced me to go along with him."

The chief just shakes his head. "There are too many problems with your story," he says, then orders his males, "Keep him and his two warriors at the point of your spears."

"You'll regret this," Ammu yells, even though he clearly has no support from the rest of the tribe. The two warriors he brought with him have dropped to their knees, arms in the air. They're not going to challenge their chief.

The chief stalks to So'Lan's open door and claps him on the shoulder.

"I didn't want to hear your words when you approached me earlier. It is a hard thing to have a long-held belief exposed as wrong. I believed in Kirokai since I was a boy. I prayed for his return. I desperately wanted him to come back and lift us up, help us.

"To hear you tell me it was just a male from a different tribe who visited from the stars. That it was a mortal, not a god, that was so hard to hear my head still hurts from it. And," he dips his chin, "my heart. But I thank you for trusting me to hear it. Trusting me not to harm the messenger. And thank you for warning me of Ammu's treacherous ways."

"Can I ask, great chief," I say. "What needs lifting up? You have the love and loyalty of your people. You have plentiful food. Everyone has lodging. Your mate is a gifted healer," I say this loud enough that she hears me. She steps closer and a small smile lights her face.

"You have clothing. You know how to make textiles and tools. You have good relations with the other tribes, so there will always be mates for your young people. You've carved out a place of safety for your tribe to live happily. What else do you need?"

His eyebrows raise in surprise, then they lower as he thinks. He lifts his hand toward our vessel. "We can't travel to the stars."

I laugh. "Many people can't, chief. It takes hundreds of generations to build up to such a thing. If it were gifted to a people before they're ready, they might misuse it." I pause for a second as I listen to what I just said. Might misuse their power? Now that I've gotten a glimpse of the galaxy, it seems more people misuse their power than not. But that's a discussion for another day.

He nods sagely. "You're right, Phoenix. We are lucky to live here. Now that I've discovered the traitor in our midst, our little village will be even safer. I thank you. For everything. Is there something we can do to help you on your way?"

"Your prayers," So'Lan says as he closes his door.

Every adult in the village has moved to the safety of the trees. They've picked up sticks and are beating them together in a unified rhythm. They're all singing. I wish I could hear them, but the vessel is airtight and no noise filters in. I see them, though.

These kind, open people took us in, helped us build a hut we'll never live in, fed us, clothed us, and believed us even though it shook the foundations of their world when we told them something they'd worshipped their whole lives was a lie.

We wave, although they can't see through our windows.

"I hope your claw does the trick, Great Kirokai." I nod toward the starter button.

He inserts the long, sharp claw on his index finger until it depresses the button, and the vessel hums to life.

"One miracle down. A thousand to go," I announce as I inspect the nav screen. Everything's in Ton'arr, but I know where we are from the star chart that flashes in green on the screen. "Let's do this!"

**So'Lan**

We take off without enough room to rise naturally. When the vessel shears off the tops of some trees, I hold onto the bottom of my seat so tightly my claws practically pierce the metal.

"Shit!" Phoenix says, but her hands stay steady on the instruments and she navigates us up and out of atmo.

"It's going to be a long trip home," she says with a frown. "This baby is doing a great job for an antique, but putting her into hyperdrive is too big a risk. We'll limp home on regular thruster power."

Home. What does that mean? My heart is still racing from today's events. From explaining my true nature to the chief, which wasn't initially well-received, to bathing him and his mate in *preniten* blood, to running through the forest wondering if at any moment Ammu's warriors were going to kill us. My thoughts were focused on protecting Phoenix.

Even now, wondering if this old machine will get us to our destination, I worry for her life.

But at this moment, my biggest worry isn't her safety, now I wonder about the future.

"Where *is* home, Phoenix?" my voice is soft.

She's already charted a course. She doesn't need to look at the nav screen, but she does, her gaze avoiding mine.

"I'll… get you back to Sanctuary." She swallows and dusts an invisible speck from the hem of her primitive shift.

At least she has the decency to act contrite.

"And you, Phoenix? Where will you go?"

"I'm a pirate. I'll have to find the credits to update this baby, then get back on track. I'm behind on some jobs."

I know I still live, but it feels as though my heart has stopped beating in my chest. Now isn't the time to talk about it, though.

"When will we arrive at Sanctuary?" I ask, keeping my voice level.

"I'm working with a handicap since neither of us read Ton'arr. I estimate five days, but it might be longer."

# Chapter Fourteen

**P**hoenix

Awkward. The last three days can only be described with that one word.

Having an elephant in the room is uncomfortable on the best of days, but in this tiny vehicle, slightly larger than a minivan, it's been painful at times.

Somehow, despite the chasm we both feel between us, we manage to put all that behind us and make love more than once a day. Make love. I shouldn't use that word, not for me at any rate. What's doubly weird about it is that it's just that—for So'Lan.

I can tell with every word he utters, every caress, every glance, that this male loves me. I just can't return it.

My life hasn't been easy. I've adopted some self-protection methods. Maybe they aren't healthy, but they work. Number one on the list is to never trust. Well, maybe that's number two. Number one is never open your heart to anyone.

In the privacy of my mind, I have to admit I've broken that rule.

We're both naked, lying in the tiny bed lodged behind the chairs. I'm still bathed in a sheen of sweat from our vigorous lovemaking. So'Smitten is sleeping with the smallest smile on his face. It's the cutest damned expression, with just the tips of his fangs peeking from between his lips.

Reaching over, I grab a slim hank of his mane and braid it. I've taken to doing this when I'm anxious, which for the past few days has been constant. I scooch closer, sling my leg around his waist to get more comfortable, and braid to my heart's content.

It makes him look amazing. There's something about him being both fierce and prettified that is sexy as hell.

I may have broken rule number one, opening my heart to him, but I can't break rule number two. I simply can't fully trust this male.

I can't deny he's saved my life a bunch of times and that I would trust him to do so again. Nor can I deny he has feelings for me. He told me he loves me. He's asked me to mate him. I know he means that as a serious commitment. I trust he's telling me his heartfelt truth.

I've climbed behind him and am squinched against the metal hull. Half his head is covered in tiny braids before I realize what my biggest objection to his proposal is. Well, it's not an objection. It's panic.

Synth.

I saw So'Lan in all his terrifying glory that first day in Dhoom's office. When I think of him, roaring and shooting me threatening looks, it sends a shiver up my spine. That probably wasn't a one-off. That's what Synth does. I have a few scars to prove it. In the height of Gant's addiction, when he ran out of his drug, he would completely lose his shit. He didn't roar, but he damn sure screamed. And hit.

So'Lan is fully detoxed. He didn't touch a drop of the tribe's fermented beverage and never asked Celletta for any of her pain-relieving herbs. When he's straight and sober, he's a worthy male. Loving, kind, thoughtful, productive. But we have to land sometime, and when we do, that evil drug will be available.

It's everywhere. The drug of choice throughout the galaxy. There's no escaping it. It's big business.

I've been asked to transport it on more than one occasion. I have no compunctions about carrying stolen goods, but I draw the line at slaves and drugs.

I can tell the moment he wakes. His lax muscles tighten as his brain comes online.

He flips around to see me, then scoots to the edge to give me more room.

"You were doing it again?" he asks as his palm inspects his head. "Half my head this time? You've been busy. What are you worried about now?" He takes both my hands and holds them steady as his big warm hands envelop mine.

How has he learned me so well in such a short time? He knows my moods as well as I do.

Should I tell him? Should I reveal my concerns? I owe it to him.

"I'll admit I have feelings for you, So'Terrific. How could I not?" I pause, having run out of gas already.

"I know." He tenderly nips the tip of my nose.

"I'm just... afraid."

He tucks me tight against him, nesting the top of my head under his chin while he caresses my back from waist to nape. He doesn't press, doesn't ask questions, just waits for me to continue.

I take a deep breath and urge myself to say it all. Like ripping off a Band-Aid, I just blurt out everything so the hard part will be over.

"The galaxy hasn't been kind to me. I've... closed myself off. With work, maybe I could open up to a wonderful male like you." His hand stutters on its journey, indicating he heard the "like you" part.

If it were me doing the listening, I would press by asking, "But?" Of course, he doesn't. He just waits me out.

"Gant, my last owner, was a Synth addict. It wasn't pretty. Have you noticed the scar on my shoulder? Gift of Gant. That's what I call them."

His fingers explore my skin and I know the moment he feels the raised scar on my right shoulder because he growls. He begins a thorough examination, his palms roving my skin, looking for more gifts from Gant.

"Top of my head," I tell him. His hands rush there and find the one-inch line where no hair grows.

"Left butt cheek."

He doesn't feel for this one. He just pulls me tighter and rocks me. You wouldn't think it would work, rocking someone lying down in this tiny space, but it does. He folds me in his arms and sways with me and kisses that spot on my head over and over. He finds a way to push his anger into the background so I don't feel like I'm the target. Instead, he comforts me.

"You saw me at my worst," he admits. "I've tried to shut out the scene from Dhoom's office, but I remember it well enough. I even remember the look on your face when you saw me. Disgust. Well, fear and disgust." He brushes more kisses to the top of my head. "I don't blame you for being terrified of me. Gant hurt you badly, and I imagine he didn't have fangs or claws like me."

"No."

"I'm over that now," he insists.

I can't help it. A little scoffing noise escapes my mouth.

"You don't believe me?" He pulls back to look at me, then tilts his head in question.

"Come on, So'Lan. You know the old adage 'once an addict, always an addict'."

"I haven't used since we crashed."

Now it's me who pulls away to look at him. "You're joking, right? You haven't had access to Synth since we crashed." Angry heat pulses through me. He's got balls to say that like it's some red badge of courage.

"Every night around the tribal fire, some of the males share potent drinks. I've never imbibed."

"Big deal. Synth is your drug of choice."

"You know firsthand that Celletta has painkilling drugs she makes from a special leaf. I saw how well it worked on you. I never asked for any."

"That doesn't mean much."

"Staying sober is easy when things are good. Would you agree it's been… stressful since our crash?" he asks.

I laugh. Stressful? The crash, the crockagators, settling into a new life, then worrying about all the moving parts of our escape.

"Yes, it's been stressful," I admit.

"Tell me one thing." He waits for me to nod. "Do you think if I'd had access to Synth I would have used it over the last few weeks?"

"Sorry, So'Lan, but yes. Absolutely."

He rolls out of bed and backs toward the two front seats, then motions me toward the rear of the ship.

"Check out the small removable panel on the back wall," he instructs from the other end of the vessel.

He was the one in charge of cleaning the ship when we found it. That must have been when he discovered the panel.

I open the square panel at head height to discover a medkit. Just like on Earth, it contains the usual suspects: gauze, tape that probably lost its stickum a century ago, and some medications. They're labeled in the Ton'arr language, but there are helpful pictures on each package for the reading impaired.

There's one with what looks like the coronavirus with a line through it. That must be an antibiotic. Then there's one with a Ton'arr face in pain, and next to it a calm face. Clearly a painkiller.

"Painkillers?" I ask.

"Not just painkillers. Some are tablets, but some are injectables."

Yep, injectables. They're in a case with indents for each injectable. Ten indents. Ten remaining vials.

"When... when did you find these?"

"The day I cleaned the ship. Weeks ago."

I stand, facing the rear panel of the ship, not wanting him to see my face. The last few weeks have been some of the most stressful of my life. The brothel, the years with Gant, they were hard. But the sheer anxiety of not knowing what the future held? The fear that's hung over my head these last few weeks? That was crushing.

It was for So'Lan too. In addition to everything terrifying me, he worried he'd be found out as a mere mortal and then killed. And he worried about me, especially after the *preniten* attack.

"You knew these were here all that time? You knew what they were?"

"I believe the labels were made for anyone to read, Phoenix. Those injectables are clearly potent painkillers."

Relief flows through me like a river. I press my head against the cool metal of the rear wall just to feel something solid against my skin. For the first time since I realized I had feelings for this handsome, fabulous male, I allow myself to believe I can find happiness with him.

"You didn't want to use them?" I ask, my voice shaky. I turn so I can read his expression.

"I thought about it once or twice. It didn't feel compelling. It was more like an echo than the real thing. I slipped into addiction because of my pain. When the physical pain was gone the emotional pain came to the forefront. I stayed there because I was demoralized. I had no hope, felt there was no reason to change. The moment I realized I loved you, I had all the motivation I needed to push those thoughts aside."

He tips his head, his gaze never leaving mine. "Phoenix, you've become my new addiction. I don't ever want to be without you."

He doesn't move. Doesn't cross the distance between us. He's not just a good male. He's patient. And smart. He knows I have to be the one to make this move.

I launch myself at him, practically flying into his embrace.

"We can do this? We can have each other?" I ask between kisses.

"We can have all of it," he rumbles into my ear.

I haven't heard him purr in a while, but his chest is vibrating now.

"Where will we live?" I ask.

"You love being a pirate. I could learn. We could be a team, flying through space."

It strikes me I've been a pirate out of necessity. It wasn't on my top five list on career day in high school. I fell into it because it kept me in the air, away from people who wanted to capture and use me. It gave me autonomy and freedom.

Is it what I want, though? Spending the rest of my life in a small ship like this? Risking not only my life but the life of the male I love?

"What would you like to do?" I almost sit down on the bed and pull him next to me, but this conversation is too big, too important to be distracted by the bed. I pull him to the front of the ship so we can sit in the seats and talk without the siren call to finish this conversation with sex.

"I'm not sure," he says with a shrug as he examines his lap.

Oh, this is new. I've never seen this expression on his gorgeous face before. Is he... shy?

"Tell me!"

He doesn't demur again. He launches, barely able to contain his enthusiasm.

"There's a gladiator arena at Sanctuary. Parts of the stands have fallen into ruin, but we've already begun to fix them. I can envision having games there. It could make money, which the compound always needs, but it excites me for other reasons."

I've seen this male full of passion before. Passion for me. But seeing his ice-blue eyes light up, his whole body energized as he talks about this. It's wonderful to watch.

"All of us gladiators in the compound were forced to fight, forced to kill. Most gladiators are slaves. It's a horrible, lonely life. But the fights themselves? They're exciting. It's how I learned to be a male. How I earned my self-esteem. I hated the killing, though.

"What if we create a place for games that have no killing? Matches that allow males who've trained their entire lives to continue to fight, just not fight to the death? There's a barracks there, Phoenix."

If I didn't know better, I'd think this was a different male than the one I've grown to know. He's sitting up straighter, his eyes are shining more brightly. He's so intense I can see that *this*, this is what he should be doing for the rest of his life.

"What if we could buy gladiators, Phoenix? Gladiator-slaves? Buy them and bring them to Sanctuary and set them free? Set. Them. Free? Just like Sanctuary was designed to be a place of refuge for Earth females, what if it could be a place of safety for gladiators?

"They would fight and win purses and decide where they want to go, what they want to do with the rest of their lives. In the meantime, they'd be safe and could save some credits."

He's talking louder now, as if he never really allowed himself to put this plan together in his head until right this minute. Maybe it's because he has me, a loving female at his side, that he's allowing all his passion, all his dreams, to come tumbling out of his mouth.

"Yes! Yes." This is doable. I want to do this with him. I want nothing more than to be part of this vision. "I want to help you. I could give up the pirate life right now, but we'll need money. Naomi will kill me for losing her statue, but at least I brought their honored, venerated hero back to them. I'll continue to make money as a pirate to fund your dream and pay back Sanctuary."

"No."

He gets up and stalks to the rear of the vessel. Is he angry? What did I say?

He uses one of his claws to pry open another panel hidden in the back wall of the ship. I hadn't seen the lines in the metal. It was well hidden.

"I discovered this the day I found the drugs. I could have returned these things to the tribe. I considered it. Maybe I'm not a good male, Phoenix, but I didn't."

When he opens the metal door of the compartment, he doesn't have to pull anything out to show me. The contents shine brightly enough for me to know exactly what that long, thin compartment is full of. Gold.

I join him at the back of the ship and together we pull out the contents of the deep compartment. Just like the tribute the tribe showered him with the first night we arrived at the village, these items are solid gold. Little crockagators and *prenitens*, and trees and leaves and a hundred other plants and animals. There are goblets and platters and jewelry.

The original Kirokai had his stash ready to go. He just never got off the ground.

"Think of each item as a gladiator," So'Lan says, his voice hushed in reverence.

We lay our booty out on the bed. There are hundreds of items, big and small.

"I can see it, So'Great. I can see all the males of different species, being bought by anonymous owners and transported to Sanctuary. I can imagine their faces as we remove their slave collars and tell them they're free. I can feel their relief when they realize they never have to fight again, that they can choose to live the rest of their lives the way they want."

## So'Lan

I'm looking out into space, imagining the things Phoenix is so richly describing. I can see the arena restored to its original greatness, but more importantly, I can see the adjoining barracks filled with happy, free males.

And I can feel the joy of being part of the team that made it happen. I can see my future and it will be wonderful.

Except, will I not be able to share it with the female I love? I may have only known her a few handfuls of days, but I know real love when it hits me. This is it. The female I've waited a lifetime to find. I've asked her to be my mate. She's excited about this project, but that means nothing because she hasn't said yes to my mating proposal.

Would the fates be so cruel as to tempt me with her? To put her in my path and dangle happiness in front of me and then have her reject me?

"You asked me to be your mate, So'Amazing. I refused so many times you put the ball in my court. On Earth, there's a proper way to perform a mating proposal. Go sit on the bed."

Really? On Earth it is done during sex? After a moment of surprise, I realize that might be a wonderful idea.

She said sit, so I ease onto the mattress and wait, never tearing my gaze from her. She moves to stand between my legs, then bends onto one knee and takes my hands in hers. Look at that. My furred hands are huge in her small pink ones. A casual onlooker would think we don't belong together. A casual onlooker would be wrong.

"So'Lan, my love."

She pauses, and I take a deep breath. She said, "my love." She's not going to reject me. Relief courses through my veins.

"I've known you less than a month. If someone had asked me a year ago if a person could not only fall in love, but know they wanted to spend the rest of their life with someone after only knowing them such a short time, I would have said they were crazy."

If my eyes were closed, my anxiety would be rising. Her words aren't meant to inspire confidence. But the love shining from her gray eyes tells me her speech is going to end well.

"I've watched your behavior through a crash, a gator attack, and a tribal coup. In all of that, I got a front-row seat to observe your character. And you are one spectacular male."

She clutches my hands more tightly.

"I had two rules to survive by, never open my heart to anyone and never trust. I broke the first rule the first time we coupled in that hut in the village. It just took my stubborn head longer to acknowledge the connection my heart has with yours.

"Trust was a tougher one to conquer. You never gave up on me. You just kept showing me in so many ways that I was safe to trust you.

"Will you be my mate? I can be moody sometimes. Well, bitchy, if you want to know the truth. In my worst moments, I can be demanding... and sarcastic. But for you, I'll try to be the best me I can be, because I love you so much, and you deserve the best."

I've watched these things on the vids the Earther females show in the dining room on Arumsday nights. This was the oddest mating proposal I've ever heard. It touches my heart because it is so... Phoenix. Raw and real and straight from the heart. Just like her.

"I would be honored to be your mate, Phoenix."

"I hope you're never So'Sorry," she laughs, then positions herself so she can wrap her arms tight around my neck. Now she kisses me with all the love and promise a kiss can convey. My arms hold her tight to my chest. I can feel our hearts beating in synchrony.

When we've had sex in the past, I held back, kept my more animal side in check. I didn't want to scare her. Before we're officially mated, she needs to see the real So'Lan in his rawest form. I can't hide my true nature from her forever. She deserves to see it now.

Breaking the kiss, I reach behind my head where her arms are clasped and bring her hands to her sides. I run my palms slowly up her arms, then gently but firmly set her away from me until she's standing in front of me, never pulling my gaze from the smokey depths of her eyes. I drop my hands to rest them on top of my knees.

"Take off your clothes," I command. My tone is deeper, as if I swallowed glass. She didn't miss my change. Her eyes flare wide. Am I mistaken, or have her lips tipped into the tiniest smile?

She shakes her beautiful head. Just one short journey to the right and then left.

"Take. Your. Clothes. Off. Or I will."

Yes. She's trying to hide it, but there's a sly smile on her lips and a look of rebellion in her eyes.

I grab her thin tribal dress at the hem and pull it up. Twisting, she tries to pull away, but there's no room to run in our little vessel. I need only take one step in any direction and I can catch her. Despite her powerful personality, she's a tiny thing compared to me.

"Before we're done today, you'll know better than to fight me," I rumble, my gaze never leaving hers.

She gasps, and for a moment, I fear I've gone too far. Am I reminding her of before? Of her bad times? One look at her face, the luminous look in her eyes, the defiant expression on her face, and I see all I need to know. She's loving this.

"Remove your bra."

When she doesn't immediately comply, I cast my voice even lower and order, "Remove it or I will rip it off."

She does, then throws it at me. She's playing this game with me. The scent of her arousal is thick in the air. I needn't worry that her mind is filled with the male who came before. She's fully present here with me.

She's called me a lion-man on many occasions. I asked her about this animal. She called it an apex predator. I feel like one now. Powerful. Mighty. Dominant.

"Pants and panties on the floor." I unsheathe my claws and point, then sweep the gold figurines off the bed and onto the floor.

She freezes for a moment. There's no movement except for her flaring nostrils. It's not in fear. She's more aroused than I've ever seen her, yet I haven't touched her. After slowly shimmying out of her clean but almost worn-out leather pants and tribal panties, she steps out of them and slowly straightens, never removing her gaze from mine.

"Hands and knees on the bed. Ass toward me," I grit out.

My cock is kicking in my pants. I can feel it leaking pre-cum. We've had sex a dozen times or more in that little hut, but neither of us has ever been this high with lust. Perhaps we've both been waiting for this.

"No," she says with a defiant shake of her beautiful head. When I take one menacing step toward her, she scrambles onto the bed but doesn't get onto all fours.

"Take inventory, little bird. Look at me, then yourself. Do you want me to force you into position?"

She looks at me with fire in her eyes. I'll take that for a yes.

I stalk to her, lift her up as if she weighs no more than one of the little golden statues, and put her in position. As much as I'm enjoying our little game, I wonder if I'll be able to last one more *minima* before I tear off my pants and sheathe myself in her.

This is too stimulating, too hot. Just a touch of my palms on her soft skin is making me regret my decision to make this coupling last for *hoaras*.

I won't be able to last long if I take off my clothes, so I keep them on. Still wearing the soft leather pants the tribe gifted me, I climb behind her on the bed and cover her.

"So'Lan," she breathes.

Is her fight gone so soon? I liked her feisty refusal to follow my orders. I'll set up another set of rules for her, then make her break them.

"Don't move," I husk into her ear. "Not one muscle. Not one word. Not even a noise. When we're done here today, I want you to know you're mine. Only mine." To emphasize my command, I wrap my tail around her waist and snug her more tightly against me.

Surprisingly, she stays perfectly still. The only noise I can hear over the steady thrum of the engine is the sound of her panting breaths.

I hump her for a moment, just to force her awareness that my body is hugging hers. That I'm huge against her small form. That I'm in command. She's gasping in tight little breaths. I know if I were to slide my finger through her folds it would come back drenched, but I don't want to give her even that much relief.

Instead, I nip the cords of her neck. She sucks in a loud breath, but I decide not to scold her. Nor do I reprimand her for the tiniest arch of her back as she tries to garner more of my touch.

I breathe hotly into her ear, then lick a path down the column of her neck. She makes a strangled noise, but immediately swallows it. I'll punish her today. Later. Not for this. This was a much smaller infraction than I'm hoping for.

My burred tongue follows the sharp line of her jaw. Her small form is swallowed underneath me. My mane brushes her cheeks. When I peer at her, I see her jaw is tightly clenched. My Phoenix likes to make noise. I discovered that in our hut.

"What a good little bird, trying so hard to follow my directions," I croon, then nip her cheek, her lips, her earlobe.

She tries to stifle a sharp intake of breath, but fails.

I give her room to follow my next direction, then say, "Open your legs."

This time, a high little squeak accompanies her compliance.

"That's good. You're doing just as I ordered." I lean over to watch her expression. Her internal debate is clear on her face. She both hates and loves my orders. I don't think even she knows which emotion is more powerful.

"Have you earned my touch?" I ask, knowing it's a trick. How can she answer, even with a head nod, when I ordered her not to move or make noise?

"Answer me."

"Yes."

My weight is on my knees and one hand as I slip one finger between her folds, practically entering her eager core. I slide it slowly toward her pleasure nub, tap it once so softly she can barely feel it, then grip her breast and pluck the bud.

She can't stifle the agonized moan of desire that punctuates my touch.

My cock punches against my pants at both her response to me and the fact she broke my rules, the rules I erected so she would break them and I could do what I'm about to do now.

"You made a noise," I announce through gritted teeth.

"Sorry. So sorry."

"And just broke my rule again."

In response to my scold, she freezes.

My mouth is at her ear as I warn, "No sound. No movement."

I pull my cock from my pants and slide it through her drenched folds.

I enjoy my ride as she stays still as a statue. For a moment, her teeth are clenched in concentration. She can't maintain that long, though. Her mouth pops open as her head tips back in pleasure.

It's torture for me, too, as I sink the tip of my cock into her tight sheath. She gasps in pleasure.

I'll have to remember this little game. It's such delicious torment for us both.

**Phoenix**

I may have only recently realized I love this guy, but I've always loved what we did together in bed. Another revelation strikes me with the force of a lightning bolt. He was slowly but steadily earning my trust even in our bed by allowing me to be in control. I could move this massive gladiator with just one finger. He never did anything without my consent or assurance that it was completely pleasurable. My heart swells even more with love and gratitude for this amazing male.

His body is perfection, and the way he moves, the way he feels, I couldn't imagine anything better.

But this? *This* is better. I loved giving myself to him, taking what I wanted, asking for more. But meeting this So'Lan, this dominant male? My channel is quivering in anticipation. There's something about his gravelly voice, his commanding tone, his forceful taking of my body that is taking me higher than I've ever been before.

I don't need to forcefully banish all remnants of my past. Gant and all the others will never invade my thoughts again. Why? Because I have So'Lan. He's wiped the slate clean.

"Suck me!" he orders

He peels himself off my back and stands. It takes a moment for my brain to come back online enough for me to follow his order.

"Now!" he thunders.

As I hop to it, I realize I'm drenched for him, and he's barely touched me.

He stands, towering over me, and points to the floor. Shit. This is so good!

I slide to my knees and look up at him. He's gorgeous, but I can't wait for him to shuck his clothes.

"Remove my pants."

Oh, I love this guy. And the orders? I'm quivering in anticipation.

A moment later, I've tugged his pants down and off. While I was doing that, he pulled off his shirt.

"Suck!"

He hasn't given me permission to speak, but I want to so badly I do it anyway.

"Yes, Sir," I snark. I can't resist. Maybe it's in my DNA, this need to push, to talk back, to fight.

"I like that. Call me Sir."

I should hate him for this, instead I feel myself moisten even more. I attack my task with gusto, licking, holding the weight of his heavy balls in one palm while I stroke him with the other. The head of his cock is slick with his desire, and I swipe it with the flat of my tongue. It's like an aphrodisiac, ramping my desire that much higher.

He's more bestial than I've ever seen him. He's not just panting, the noise is coming out in a lion-like growl.

"Stop!" he orders.

He was an inch from coming. I imagine he has another idea in mind for where he wants that to happen.

"Lay on the bed. On your back. Pull your legs up and hold your hands behind your knees."

When I'm in position, he stops all motion and drinks in the sight of me. I think he was about to plunge into me, but seeing me like this. Open. Obedient. Wanting. Maybe it told him in a more primitive manner than my mating proposal that I want him. That I'll take him, take all of him in whatever way he wants to be with me.

All the dominance seems to bleed from him as he pulls me to the edge of the bed, hits his knees, and laps at me. The role reversal stuns me, then brings tears to my eyes.

This is us. In all our glory. I can be me with him, whether I'm my piratical self, giving orders, or my feminine self, taking them. And he can be So'Lan. I loved his dominance, and can't wait to meet that part of him again—soon! But I love this So'Lan, too. Worshipping at the altar of my pussy. How could I say no to that?

Five or six orgasms later—it's hard to know when they cluster together so fast and furious—he rises to mount me.

"I love you, Phoenix," he says with more passion than ever before. His blue eyes are darker than I've ever seen them. Usually ice-blue, bordering on aquamarine, right now they're the color of Earth's sky before a spring rain. They're full of affection.

My heart squeezes with an echoing feeling of love as I pay attention to every moment. Maybe we'll have a ceremony somewhere in the future, but I think we both know this is it. *This* is the real ceremony. When he pierces into me, we'll be bound forever.

I've bared myself to him. There's no reason to hold any part of me back, so I feel compelled to say it.

"So'Lan. So'Mate." It strikes me as perfect to say, "Soulmate."

Perhaps he was waiting for that, because he presses into me as if he wants this moment to last forever. He's long and thick and his entry stretches me in a way that reminds me he owns my heart.

The sweetness of the moment passes swiftly into passion. Now that he's entered me, he can't hold back. He's pounding into me. Pistoning hard and fast as a machine. I feel his balls swinging against my back hole and his pelvic bone pressing against my clit.

I lift to scrape my nipples along his furred chest, then throw my arms around his neck so we can't separate. I bite his cheeks and kiss his lips and my heart opens even wider when I see his fangs, bared to the gums. It's a true statement of our comfort level. He doesn't have to hide any aspect of his authentic self from me. Nor me him.

He dips his head and bites the juncture where my neck meets my shoulder. This isn't like the thousand nips he's given me in the past. This is a bite. His fangs pierce my flesh and make me grunt in pain. I didn't expect this. But the pain miraculously turns to pleasure and my orgasm rushes at me hard and fast like a fire stallion from Aeon II.

"So'Lan!"

I hold onto his shoulders, clutching for dear life, feeling if I let go I'll tumble into space. His haunches tighten as he thrusts into me once more, so hard it makes my teeth clack together. I feel his hot essence bathe my inner walls, knowing we're truly joined.

He releases his jaw from my shoulder, then roars. It's not a shy release of sound. It's loud and long and so deep the golden statues we tossed on the floor are vibrating with the noise. He roars once more, pointing his mouth away from me so he doesn't hurt my ears, but it's beautiful.

"So'Sexy. So'Mine!" Oh, he is so mine.

He licks my shoulder. Something in his saliva removes the sting.

"That's going to leave a mark." He tips his head sheepishly but can't hide the pride shining from his eyes or his smile of satisfaction.

"Yes. A clear mark of ownership," I admit. "And you? I want all those pretty females out there to know you're spoken for."

"I know just the thing," he says, then snugs me tight. "Of all the ways you've mangled my name, there's one I like the best."

He waits for me to raise an eyebrow in question.

"So'Mine."

# Epilogue

**O**ne Year Later
**Phoenix**

It's been a year in the making, but we're finally here. I wanted to wear something special, so I hunted all over the Intergalactic Database to find a picture of what I wanted.

It took a village to sew this thing. I know nothing about sewing and had to enlist the help of all my new friends here at Sanctuary. We had a blast designing and creating it. Every woman in the compound is wearing a variation on the theme, all in different colors.

The design reminds me of a Roman dress that sweeps to the floor. It exposes one shoulder. I specifically wanted this design because it bares the shoulder where I wear my mate mark with pride. I chose crimson because it will look so beautiful against So'Lan's golden fur when I stand next to him.

As I look around, I feel like I'm back in ancient Rome. I'm sitting high on the stone steps ringing the arena in Sanctuary. So'Lan was right. It was in disrepair when we first touched down after our return from the asteroid.

Everyone was so happy to see us. We'd been out of communication for weeks. Thantose knew I had an SOS buoy, but since there was no trace of a signal, they assumed we were dead. I heard Naomi and Dhoom, not knowing the details, assumed So'Lan was the cause of our demise and felt terrible about hiring me to take So'Lan to Kryton.

They were relieved he wasn't the cause of the crash, and in fact had recovered from his Synth addiction. They still felt somehow responsible for our misadventure in spite of the "all's well that ends well" result.

To relieve their guilt, it took me a while to bare my shoulders. There's a doozy of a scar on one shoulder from the awful monkey bite, but the other shoulder exposes my pride and joy—four white marks where his fangs pierced me. He takes care to always bite the same place when we feel the need to reenact our little marking ceremony. It always makes me come so hard I can't stifle my screams of pleasure.

I turn my attention back to the crowd. I've made friends here. Everyone was thrilled when we returned, and so happy their esteemed friend came back a changed male. All the females wanted to get to know me and make me feel welcomed. I have a family for the first time since I left Earth. I love it here.

When we showed everyone the golden statues and told them of So'Lan's dream to rescue gladiators, give them a home, and host non-lethal fights in the arena, it was the first time anyone had ever seen Naomi cry. She didn't even mention losing the sale on the Dacian statue.

Shortly after we returned to Sanctuary, So'Lan admitted the feelings of fear I thought I kept hidden by my bravado never fooled him. Being here, in a compound where we've all got each other's back, has helped me banish all the fear that used to swirl just under my surface. Having the love of my life by my side put most of my anxieties to rest.

So'Lan and I got to work right away. First, we cleaned and renovated one of the tiny stone houses on the periphery of the action. It's not much bigger than our hut on the asteroid, but it's bright and homey and perfect for our needs. I couldn't ask for anything better. So'Lan and I have already drawn up plans for how to expand it when we have a child—a kit as he calls them.

"May I have your attention!" So'Lan's voice booms over the loudspeakers. I'm sitting on the steps. He's in the announcer's booth that towers over the large arena.

"I want to welcome you all for coming to the first games in our new stadium. Thanks to all who have helped us transform this from dream to reality, working tirelessly over the last *annum*. The seats have been patched to look like new and this announcer's booth now has the latest equipment.

"Yes, the stadium itself has experienced quite an overhaul, but it's what's inside that merits more discussion. My beloved mate Phoenix and I have been supported by every female and male in this compound in our efforts to make Sanctuary a true sanctuary for females *and* males."

I smile, picturing his face as he talks. Perhaps no one else in the stands suspects, but I'm pretty sure his eyes are watering with emotion.

"We've always wanted this place to be a safe haven for abducted Earth females, but my dream of freeing gladiator-slaves has now come to fruition."

Everyone in the arena stands and claps. Thantose and the crew from the *Ataraxia* are here, and not one but two ships of freed gladiators and their human mates. They're the ones who killed Daneur Khour and freed almost everyone in Sanctuary. They're all beaming with happiness at what we've created.

When their applause dies down, they continue standing as So'Lan says, "In the past *annum*, we have renovated the barracks, and it now houses five gladiators."

He's interrupted by more applause. Through the din, he says, "Stand on your seats, please. We all know who you are, but stand so we may cheer you!"

The five males we've rescued, each costing a single golden statue, stand on the stone benches they had been sitting on. A few are surprisingly shy, the others lift their arms to soak in their adulation. They may be free, but they're still gladiators, after all.

"With the stadium now fully renovated, I'd like to give it a fitting name."

I knew he'd hired stonecutters from the nearby fair to come the other day and chip off the old name that was so weather-worn it was unreadable. They chiseled in a new name, then covered it with a tarp.

My cheeks begin to heat when he launches into the tale of the phoenix and its promise of rising from the ashes. It held special meaning for me, so much that I took it for my name, but it holds meaning for every one of us in this arena. We have all experienced pain and hardship, and we have all risen to find meaningful lives filled with purpose. Some of us have found love. I hope every single person who hasn't will find it in their own time.

"I hereby name this the Phoenix Stadium."

Everyone in the stadium climbs onto their stone seat and cheers.

"Please enjoy the banquet laid out on the lower level of the arena. It is my wish that no blood ever seeps into the sand, but feel free to drip all the crumbs you want," he says, then stalks out of the booth. I can see his expression from here. He's so proud of himself, his fangs are shining white in the sunlight in all their ferocious glory.

Will I ever be able to look at him and not think he's the most handsome male I've ever met? Probably not.

I wear my mating mark proudly, but he wears my love for him just as visibly. We melted down the statue of the *megasto*. Who wanted a reminder of those horrid crockagator beasts? Dhoom helped us form the smelted gold into beads, and I braid them into his hair.

Although my anxiety melted away shortly after we touched down back on Sanctuary, I still love to braid my male's hair. I love the way the beads tinkle softly when he moves his head. The sound accompanies our lovemaking when we're vigorous. It's better than a wedding ring, announcing to anyone with eyes that the beautiful lion-man's heart belongs to me.

Well, that and his bellowing mating roar that manifests when a Ton'arr male releases with his life's truemate. No matter how far away our cottage is from the main buildings, we get funny looks the morning after we have sex. Which is, well, every morning.

We wait for everyone else to walk down the stone steps toward the tables below that are laden with a banquet full of food.

We hold each other as we gaze into each other's eyes.

"You kept a secret pretty well, So'Mine."

"Aye, little bird. What can I say? You picked the name first, but it describes each and every one of our stories."

I rise on my toes to kiss him.

"Let's grab some food before it's all gone, then we've got work to do. I put an anonymous bid in on a Halckon gladiator who's up for sale on Galgon," he says. "We're a few hours away from buying our next resident."

## So'Lan

I know we should make our way to the sands below and laugh and congratulate all our friends for our very good fortune, but I just want to bask in this feeling for a moment.

I turn Phoenix in my arms so her back presses against my front. As always, I marvel at how small she is against me. At first glance, anyone would think we're the last two people in the galaxy to belong together, but they're wrong.

We're perfect together.

She's a fiery feisty female who can go toe to toe with any of the gladiators in the compound, even if it's only in spirit.

In our bed, she loves to give her power to me. Except when she doesn't. It's fun to be at my powerful female's mercy at times. It's all a game where no matter how we play it, we both win. Every. Single. Time.

"Happy, my love?" she asks.

"Happier than I ever thought possible, little bird. And you?"

"You're about to get happier, So'Mine. We need to find time to make those renovations to our house." She waggles an eyebrow at me.

"You're going to have a kit?" I didn't think I could be any happier, but my heart explodes in joy.

"I'm pretty sure, but maybe we should hurry back to our cabin just to ensure we get it right."

"You're a tease. Teasers get punished."

"Can't wait."

# Dear Reader

I had a lot of fun writing this So'Sexy, So'Exciting book. I hope you enjoyed reading it.

By the way, not only is this book five in the Galaxy Sanctuary Series, but check out the 17 book prequel series: Galaxy Gladiators! Or the four book sister series: Galaxy Pirates. Sister series? Is that a thing? Would it be brother series? I don't know, but check it out.

Hugs,

Alana

# SNEAK PEEK DHOOM: BOOK FIVE IN THE GALAXY SANCTUARY SERIES

**P**resent Day

**On Planet Fairea in the Sanctuary Compound**

**Chapter One**

**Dhoom**

I hate this. Which isn't to say I don't deserve it. If this were my punishment for every unforgivable thing I've done, it would mean I've gotten off far too easy. Still, I can't stand this.

"See?" Naomi points to the computer screen on her desk. "I just can't see how these numbers make sense. I wish Juno were here. She's got a head for figures."

We're in Naomi's office here on Sanctuary. A little less than an *annum* ago, we were all slaves here at Daneur Khour's enormous compound. He was the head of the largest, most dangerous cartel in the galaxy.

He held me, along with seven other gladiators, in an underground dungeon as punishment for what he referred to as "underperforming." Naomi and several Earther females were held here too. They were in less oppressive accommodations aboveground, but were slaves nonetheless.

Some gladiators who also had a grudge against the evil bastard infiltrated the massive compound, killed Khour and his staff, and freed us all. Since then, Naomi has overseen money, purchases, and concerns about the females. I somehow became the *de facto* head of the males. It wasn't the result of a vote, it just kind of… happened.

I leave most of the day-to-day decisions to Naomi. She has the mind and temperament for it. I always thought these things came easily to her, so I was surprised when she comm'd and asked me to help her sort through a math problem. Usually Juno is here to assist with accounting issues, but she's off-planet with her mate, Abraxx.

So here I am, standing behind Naomi, who is at the largest desk I've ever seen. It's a remnant from Khour's reign. This, in fact, is his old office. Although we've sold off some of the expensive trinkets that used to cover the built-in shelves, the room is still opulent, elegant, and large enough to easily house a family of four.

As Naomi scrolls through pages of figures, I lean forward, trying to make sense of them.

"Naomi, perhaps you could wait until Juno—"

"This can't wait. I need to sort through it. Somehow, we've lost over a hundred thousand credits. We work too hard for our money to have it disappear." She leans closer to the screen as if that will provide the answers she's looking for.

This is pure Naomi. We've known each other for an *annum*. She's a strong-willed female, probably the most commanding one I've ever known. She runs Sanctuary by the sheer force of her will. She's brought us from poverty to a strong financial position, but she always says we need more if we're going to survive.

The gladiators who rescued us killed Khour and helped us forge ownership papers for the property, but we know it's just a matter of time before the powerful MarZan cartel comes to take their property back. We thought we were finally safe a few *lunars* months ago when So'Lan and Phoenix brought back millions in gold. Little did we know the missile defense system we installed would be obsolete so fast we're already in desperate need of an upgrade to defend ourselves from attack.

Naomi worries about this and is desperate for ways, legal or not, to accumulate the funds we need. She's the one person who coordinates everyone and every purchase or sale to keep this compound running. This is her way of caring for us. She certainly doesn't show her concern in other, warmer ways.

The two of us used to butt heads, but we've developed an uneasy truce. The others in the compound hated it when we argued. We've discovered ways to get along, which usually involve me agreeing to her wishes. I only intervene when she's being too harsh with the others.

Her motives are in the right place. We call this place Sanctuary because we've built it to provide asylum for escaped slaves. It's a beacon of hope for the downtrodden across the galaxy. But, as Naomi would be the first to tell you, that costs money.

"Here." She points to the screen. "I don't know what's wrong, but I think it's in this column of figures."

I lean so my head is next to hers, but nothing pops out at me.

I don't believe I've ever been this close to Naomi before. For the first time, I'm aware of Naomi not as my nemesis, but as a female. Perhaps it's the way she smells. Her fresh, clean scent wafts into my nostrils and draws my attention.

After taking one step back, I pretend to focus on the screen, but I've moved to get a better view of her. I don't know why, after knowing her all these *lunars*, I've become aware of her as a female, but I'm looking at her in a new way.

Her brown hair, as usual, is pulled to her nape in a severe bun. Perhaps because it's been a long day, her usually straight hair has escaped into tendrils now framing the delicate features of her face. She tips her head to the side as her top teeth worry her plump bottom lip. I imagine her mouth doing other things. Sexual things.

I was in that dungeon for almost two *annums* and have been out for one. In that time, I haven't had sex, haven't wanted to. I've been doing a good job of punishing myself and my strict no-sex edict is part of my strategy.

I take a deep but subtle breath in through my nose, drinking in Naomi's unique scent. I don't feel guilty about it. It's a clever way for me to abuse myself by reminding myself I'm a male while at the same time maintaining my vow to never have a female. I don't deserve one.

"Naomi," Dawn's urgent voice interrupts on comms. "Jaggard is here with the shipment of seeds. He's demanding payment of 450 credits per bag, but I thought you negotiated it at 400."

"Shit," Naomi says as she breathes deeply through her nose and closes her eyes. It's as if she's trying to control her temper. "I'll be right back."

As she leaves to take care of business, I notice for the first time how gracefully she moves. Have we really shared meals together and argued through meeting after meeting, and I've never noticed how perfect her figure is?

She's not a young female like the other Earthers. I've never asked her story, but it's clear she was abducted *annums* ago. She reads, writes, and speaks fluent Universal and, from what I've observed, was one of Khour's most trusted slaves for *annums*.

I should have asked about her history long ago. Perhaps knowing more about her would have helped us bridge the gaps between us. Maybe it would have explained this female's sheer drive and determination to make Sanctuary a safe haven for slaves across the galaxy.

I've let her carry the burden since the beginning, only helping when called upon. It's just one more reason I deserve punishment.

I take this moment to decide to step up. No longer will all the work fall on Naomi's shoulders.

Sliding into her chair, I lean forward to parse through these figures. I may not have had formal education past age ten, may not understand higher mathematics, but I understand numbers. If Naomi thinks there's a problem here, I'm going to help her find it.

I've grown accustomed to using a computer, but I've always preferred to do this the old-fashioned way. Rummaging in the top right desk drawer, I look for a writing utensil and paper. I'm not surprised the contents are neat and orderly. I would expect nothing else from Naomi.

What does surprise me, though, is the size of the drawer.

This is Daneur Khour's desk, or at least it was before our friends ended his miserable life. It's large, imposing, made to give the impression the owner wields power. It's beautiful, made of some unknown rich, brown, burled wood that matches the room's paneled walls.

Intrigued, I slide to my knees and inspect the pillar of stacked drawers. From the outside, they look like they run the entire five-*fierto* width of the desk. When I pull them out, the bottom two drawers fit the size of the desk. This top drawer, though, is only three *fiertos* long.

Khour was a male who loved secrets and elaborate puzzles. We've found many things secreted away on this compound. I think I've just found another.

Lying on my back, I investigate with my fingertips. I find seams where the wood has an almost-imperceptible joint, although none is needed. It takes a moment more of prodding and poking before I discover that pressing in and then up opens a hidden panel.

When I draw it away, I see a metal safe.

"Dhoom, I—" Naomi says as she barges through the door. "Shit," she sighs. "I shouldn't be surprised he bailed on me."

"Down here," I call as I stifle my irritation. I've abandoned her dozens of times since we've taken leadership roles, leaving her alone to sort things out time and again. No wonder she leaped to the conclusion I left her to clean up this mess.

**Naomi**

Has he fallen? Had a seizure? What's he doing under the desk? Perhaps he was too out of it to notice my bitchy comment when I assumed he'd bailed on me. I've been trying to be nicer to everyone, although it doesn't come easily to me.

"Look," he says when I round the desk.

Dhoom is a big male, and like all the gladiators in the compound, he prefers wearing a simple loincloth to actual clothes. He's on his back under the desk, knees bent, with all his glorious ** flesh displayed for me to see.

I spend more time with him than any other male on the premises. We used to have screaming matches, but several of the women said our fights scared them. I've spent my entire adult life sucking it up and kissing Daneur Khour's ass. I guess when I finally got a chance to assert myself, I went overboard, but everyone here has been traumatized. I don't want my behavior to compound that.

Dhoom and I don't fight much anymore, but we're barely civil. That doesn't mean I haven't noticed his body. All the males in the compound were gladiators. They spent decades honing their bodies into perfect fighting machines. Emphasis on the word perfect. A woman would have to be deaf and blind not to notice.

But there's something about Dhoom that has always appealed to me. Maybe it's because he's the oldest male here, as I'm the oldest female. Maybe it's that I'd vote him most likely to kill someone with his bare hands.

He's the scariest male I've ever seen. That's saying a lot, considering I worked for Khour for decades. As the head of the galaxy's most powerful cartel, he rubbed elbows with some of the most evil assholes out there.

No one looked more imposing than Dhoom. **description**

Dropping to my knees, I crawl into the dark confines under the desk. I feel dwarfed next to his huge powerful body, but try to keep my attention on where he's pointing.

"There was a hidden panel. Here's a safe."

"I'm not surprised," I say, even as I wonder why I hadn't examined the desk more thoroughly in the year I've sat here.

Khour was crazy like a fox and paranoid as a shithouse rat. He trusted no one and kept layers of secrecy even from people like me who had access to some of his most private information.

No. It doesn't surprise me he had a hidden compartment right under my nose. Whatever is in here is important. We've found a few other safes, one in his bedroom, another in the wall of this office, but here, near his cock and balls, I imagine there's a treasure trove of money or important information.

"We'll have to find a locksmith," I say, even as I hate the idea. Locksmiths mean outsiders. Outsiders mean jeopardy.

Every day I wake up wondering when Khour's replacement is going to rain down the fires of hell upon our compound. The only reason I think we've escaped their notice this long is that his people are still killing each other as they jockey for position within the organization.

Dhoom is proving to be a distraction as I lie here, trying to think. Not only is his big body radiating heat like a furnace, but his spicy masculine scent is seeping into my nostrils. I scoot out from under the desk and try to focus.

Dhoom slides out, the thin wooden panel he removed from the desk still in his grip.

Now that it's out in the light, I see some writing on the interior of the panel. I don't allow myself to feel excited, not even for a moment. Khour never would have been so dumb, so obvious, as to write the combination right there. That would be a rookie mistake and unworthy of a criminal mastermind. He was the meanest male in the galaxy, but he was far from dumb.

Dhoom and I are sitting hip to hip and we each grasp a side of the panel. There's writing here, all right.

"Numbers. Could he have been so dumb as to write the combination here?" Dhoom asks.

"There are too many numbers to be a combination," I say.

"Bank account?" he asks.

"Gee, I hope not."

I'm sure we're both thinking of seven months ago when Dawn and Revikk went to planet Morgana to grift money out of one of Khour's accounts. They were seconds away from dying a couple of times on that little caper. I'd hoped we'd never have to do anything like that again.

I stand, ease back into my chair, and input the numbers into the Intergalactic Database. I'm not surprised when nothing helpful comes up.

With a little more searching, though, I think I figure out what we've got.

"Geographic coordinates," Dhoom says, a hair's breadth from my ear a moment before I say it out loud.

It doesn't take long before we pinpoint the coordinates and realize it's right here on our property.

"Too easy," I breathe. "We're definitely going to pursue this, but he was too clever, too devious to put the key to the combination almost in plain sight."

"Aye. You'd almost think it was a trap," he husks, his warm breath ruffling my hair.

"I have a feeling whatever's in here is important," I say. "I want to investigate tomorrow."

"We've found other valuables, but this, right next to his cock, I think it held special meaning," he says.

It's interesting how much we think alike.

"But *you* are not investigating tomorrow," he says. "Too dangerous. I'll go."

For half a second, I think he might want to beat me to the coordinates to get his hands on the treasure. But we're a team. All of us on Sanctuary have been working together for almost a year. He wouldn't be trying to cheat us out of an asset belonging to everyone. Would he?

"We'll both go," I say, my voice clipped. "I'll meet you in the hangar at nine."

# Acknowledgements

T hanks to my tribe! It takes a village to write a book.

I have my super early readers who get dailies of my writing: Dr. Lee, who I call my Developmental Editor, and my assistant Stephanie. They tell me if I'm going in the wrong direction and make sure my heroes are sexy, my heroines are loveable, and I fill the book with enough action and spice to keep my readers happy.

As always thanks to my daughter, Amarra Skye, an author in her own right who never fails to help with plotting. Also huge thanks to my friend Kassie Keegan who helps with werdzing in many ways.

My alpha and beta teams get the book after I've completed it and they give me feedback along the way. They are: Karen H., Kathy F., Christine R., Sarah B., Jhane M., Kimber J., Lorraine B., Patricia M., Shannon B., Anne-Marie S., Corda A., Kaye S., Vedece B., Marianne K., Sue P., Anuschka-Marie W., Kimberley F.

And a big thank you to my Patron Katrine A.

# Λbout Λlaηλ Khλη

Do you really want to know I have the cutest ragdoll cat in the world? Aren't you more interested in the sexy books I write for fun?

My sexy heroes inhabit my dreams and insist I put their love stories on the page. Most of my books happen in outer space, but the emotions and struggles could happen to anyone. Well, not the villains who look like snakes, or the spaceships, or the lion-men, or… well, okay, maybe none of this could happen to you. But you can go there with me when you read my books.

Join my newsletter for cover reveals, free chapters, deleted scenes, and weekly giveaways. **www.alanakhan.com**

**https://www.facebook.com/khanstribe**

**https://www.amazon.com/Alana-Khan/e/B07S1CFFXP/ref=dp_byline_cont_pop_ebooks_1**

# Also By Alana Khan

Vartan

Maximus

Steele

Tarrex

**An Alien Rescue Romance**

Jax-Xon

**Galaxy Sanctuary Alien Abduction Romance Series**

Thran

Abraxx

Revikk

So'Lan

**Galaxy Games Hostile Planet Series**

**(written as Anna Lynn)**

Down To One

**Cosmic Kissed (Earthbound Alien Romance Series)**

Love On Impact

Love Uncaged

**Galaxy Pirates Alien Abduction Romance Series**

Sextus

Thantose

Ssly

Slag

**Mastered by the Zinn Alien Abduction Romance Series**

Voxx 1

Voxx 2

Voxx 3

**Treasured by the Zinn Alien Abduction Romance Series**

Arzz

Trev

Sinn

**Billionaire Doms of Blackstone**

**(written as Deja Blue)**

Direct Me

Heal Me

Instruct Me

Teach Me

**Charity Anthology**

Claimed Among The Stars

**Box Sets**

Galaxy Gladiators Alien Abduction Romance Series Books 1 to 3

Galaxy Gladiators Alien Abduction Romance Series Books 1 to 4

First In Series - Zar / Sextus / Arzz

Galaxy Pirates Alien Abduction Romance Series Books 1 to 4

Treasured by the Zinn Alien Abduction Romance Series

Mastered by the Zinn Alien Abduction Romance Series

Printed in Great Britain
by Amazon

75543568R00135